SWELLEN'S ORPHANS

by
W. HOCK HOCHHEIM

Page 2

Paperback ISBN: 979-8-9898150-1-2
Audio Book ISBN

Other Titles by W. Hock Hochheim
Fightin' Words
Knife Combatives
Impact Weapon
Combatives Footwork and Maneuvering
My Gun is My Passport
Last of the Gunmen
Rio Grande Black Magic
American Medieval
Blood Rust
The China Alamo
Kill Them Back
Face the Muzak
Takedown the Take
The Great Escapes of Pancho Villa
Training Mission Series 1-5

TABLE OF CONTENTS

Prologue

In 1880 Joe Juneau discovered gold in the Silverbow Basin of Alaska. In 1886, Howard Franklin and Henry Madison struck gold on Fortymile River in the interior of Alaska near the Canadian border. These discoveries, and subsequent discoveries in the Klondike, Yukon region, and nearby, prompted thousands of dreamers to migrate into the northwest territories with hopes to strike it rich through the 1880s and 1890s to find gold, or support those that found gold or at least tried.

In 1893, so did the wanted dead or alive fugitive and former Lt. General, Mordecai "Swoop" Swellen, until…

Chapter 1: Ed June, Be the Death Of

Owyhee, the Canyonlands, the Great Basin Desert of Northern Idaho…

Bullets cracked the air and zipped by his ears. Swoop Swellen worried about how long, how far, and how fast his horse could race at this pace across the rocky and sandy high desert in the western region of Oregon's Owyhee Canyonlands. The ground was patched with soft sand and hard rock packed with parts of crevices, drops and climbs. The five Wells Fargo agents were now galloping behind him and just within pistol range.

Swoop worried too, what if a round hit his horse? What if a river or deep canyon suddenly appeared ahead, terrain once hidden by the flat, blurry, heat waves off the summer broiling grounds? How did they know to chase him so damn soon when he fled Portland in the middle of the night?

He, like so many people migrated to the magnetic lure

of gold in the greater Northwest and Alaska. But you need not just be the classic prospector to achieve some financial success within any gold or silver boom. There were many support jobs. Prospectors need supplies, food, some lodging, and "entertainment" of all sorts – some wild pastimes - and that includes the oddest desires of mankind, sometimes the oddest of sordid taboos.

A gold rush operation also required law enforcement and security. Lots of it. The rush survived on extensive protection services. When gold is actually located and mined, it needs transportation from storage by foot, mule, horse, wagon, boat and, or train.

In the winter of 1893, an ambitious time to travel and live in the "Last Frontier" and thereabouts, Swoop worked for Wilderman Security under the name of Edward June guarding wagons and trains carrying the ore. Invariably, a slice of these guards were bad apples and were involved in illegal plots and thefts, sometimes brilliant, sometimes very stupid. Gold in all its forms magically disappeared from time to time, very often abetted by insider information needed to pull off such capers.

Before long, the pan-pick-and-shovel miners, the transporters, the assayers, the rich, the mining companies, the banks and their insurance companies demanded that investigators like those from the Pinkertons and Wells Fargo discover what had happened to their percentages of lost treasure. Armed with stacks of the newest wanted posters, the enforcers arrived with announced plans for investigating every employee. With this news, Swoop knew he simply had to depart. No doubt his Army wanted poster would be in a stack.

So, just before his scheduled interview and examination, Swoop bought a horse and took off for the East. This sudden, untimely departure-escape sparked even more enquiry.

"Where's this Ed June feller?"

"They say he be gone. Two, three nights ago."

Several agents compared wanted posters with him.

"I'll be a hog's swaller' if that ain't him," one agent said.

"You mean the renegade general? Him?"

"Hells bells, yes. Look at that face. Righteous height. Righteous weight. Come on, cipher through it. It's him."

"I think you're right," a third agent said.

"It all fits and with him leavin' so fast and all. I say we run after him. The bounty is $1,000."

"We could split it five ways!" one said.

"Six. Remember, Wells Fargo gets a share too. They're happy when we collect a bounty. Money fer' them, too."

As the bullets flew, Swoop concluded from their fervor, that he was also chased by bounty hunters or the authorities for far more than just dodging a routine questioning. They must have discovered who he really was.

He considered he might stop suddenly and short, try to coerce his mount to lay down on its side, into a common Army cavalry horse's last stand. He'd also get down behind the prone horse, rifle out and start shooting back. But this horse? Was it trained for such a quick combat move? Probably not.

How long would such a stop and setup take? Would the horse go down and stay down? And if these are Wells Fargo agents or Pinkertons, they are often veterans, ex-lawmen, and, or scoundrels of violence themselves. How long before they just outflank him with cover fire? Plus, he did not hanker to kill these men, just blindly doing their job. Maybe just ahead there was some geography he might use to outsmart and escape? So far? Nothing. Desperate, he raced on.

But then a trench! Just ahead! A deep, thin, dry stream, a crack in the ground about 6 feet wide appeared in a sudden view, yet his horse took it all in stride, the drum of her hooves stopped as they flew through the air, to pick up the pounding again on the other side.

"Atta' girl! Maybe that cranny will slow them down some," Swoop said aloud.

But the passing crack of bullets still told the tale that these mysterious pursuers were still in handgun range, even with the trench.

Then the worst thing happened. The poor horse was shot in the rear. Twice. Bullets tore through her hind quarters so deep, her speed decreased so quickly down to much less than half speed and an erratic, stumbling limp. And that shutdown was all it took for Swoop to go flying, airborne forward over the mare's head and spinning him through the air like a circus acrobat. With no net. And that flight was the last he remembered…

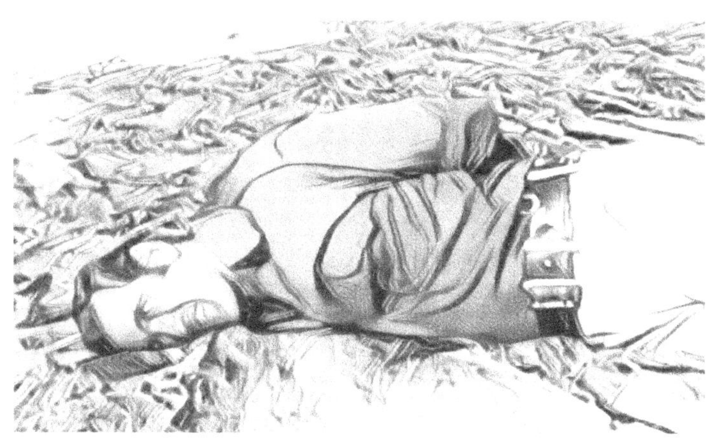

Chapter 2: Sugar Bowl Thomas, the Agent

Swoop woke up for a second when someone dropped him on the ground. He passed out again. He woke up for another second or two when someone kicked him. He passed out again. Then the third time, he woke up and remained so, in pain, groggy and confused.

"Welllll, good morning General Sunshine."

Swoop coughed and looked at the man's face leaning into him and about 5 feet away. Swoop found himself almost prone on a slight slope of dirt, and he reflexively tried to yank his hands from behind his back, but they were tied, along with his ankles too. He looked at his feet. His boots were removed.

Then he looked around to see four other men walking about or seated on the ground near a campfire. He could smell coffee and bacon. Horses were lined up to the far left tied off by a long rope between two scrub bushes.

"We're Wells Fargo agents, Generalissimo. Back there, your horse fell, General. Then you fell," the man said.

"Looong ways," and he lofted his hand in the air, up over and down. "Heaaaad first landing. Boom."

"Why you calling me, General? Ahhh, you…the horse?

My horse…"

"She's dead. Bout' rolled over the top of ya'," he said. "You flew and she fell. My name's Thomas. "Sugar Bowl" Thomas. Wells Fargo. We is all Wells Fargo here." Sugar Thomas leaned further in. "Yer' still bleeding a little. Yup. When you Mister General, when you disappeared from Portland, we got extra suspicious of you. We always have a passel of new wanted posters when we get dispatched somewhere. Everyone at Wilderman Security said the renegade general poster was you when they'd seen it. Had to be you. We'd have to agree."

"I didn't steal any gold dust," Swoop mumbled.

"Oh, I know. We know. You is a good boy, cept' for being a traitor to our country. They all vouched for you as a good feller at Wilderman. Helpful and wise in setting things up. Like a general might be, actually. But you did have over $200 cash in your saddlebags."

"My…my life savings," Swoop said.

"Ohhhh? Oh. What a life then, huh?"

"Why don't you fellers just take that money and let me go?" Swoop said, loud enough for all of them to hear. And he looked them over to make sure.

"Two hundred dollars? Only? We be thinking that we'll be a keepin' that $200 anyway AND still get the $1,000 Army RE-ward atop it. Killin ya' helps us keep the $200. We be a keepin' all that money."

Swoop grimaced at the word "killing." He was feeling faint and sick to his stomach.

"That's right, Mister General Sunshine. One thousand, two hundreds split five ways."

"Six ways fer the $1,000, Sugar!" another agent near the fire called out in a frustrated voice.

"Yeah, six ways. Hey, that bacon smells good, huh? But here's our problem, a bacon supply problem, well, your problem. You see, you are wanted dead or alive. It would be a lot easier if'n we just kilt' you right here. Right now, I mean why should we be feedin' an eventual dead man? And certain said dead feller - you - all over Oregon to the authorities?"

"Army happy to hear you found the general?" Swoop asked.

"Oh, we ain't told em' yet. We don't want them charging out here after you, taking you and keeping that $1,000."

"Smart. But still dumb Thomas Sugar…Bowl. Uh-huh. Your real problem is," Swoop said, "ain't feeding me bacon. I ain't this general y'all are looking for. You already know my name is Edward June. So, smart you haven't called the Army."

"Zat' so?"

'That's so," Swoop said, already thinking about a plan to stay alive. "Smart because, I ain't your general."

"Ha! Zats' so? Why you run then?"

"I left to wander east. Tired of the work. Back, two mornings ago…been two mornings?"

"Been two," Sugar Bowl said.

"I thought you were some strangers," Swoop continued, "all of a sudden shooting at me like that. I thought you were bushwhackers. And you are! You did bush me! Look at me, all tied up," Swoop said, "talking about killing me, cold."

"HA! You say."

"Ha, I say!" Swoop said.

The other four turned their heads to fully watch and listen in.

"I have been mistaken for this…this general once before. In Balch Springs, Texas. Some idiots rounded me up down there, took me to the city jail and called the Army in. Couple of Army officers walked in, they took a look at me and let me go. One of them knew the real general. When you do call the Army, ask them if they know Ed June. Edward June from Illinois and this fandango in Balch Springs."

"The hell you say," and he kicked Swoop in the thigh.

"The hell I do say. And THAT is why you'd better not kill me. I ain't him. He ain't me."

The man curled his lip. The others just continued to stare at them.

"You kill me for no reason? They'll hang you all for murder, you kill me. Yeah," Swoop said.

"I tell you what…" Sugar Bowl Thomas started, but… he couldn't finish. There was a little zipping sound and small, "thunk" sound. Next there was an arrow in Sugar Bowl Thomas' head!

In one second or less, while Swoop was looking at him and an arrow landed right into the left side of his head. He stood there for that second, went cross-eyed, made an odd face, and he dropped dead right atop Swoop.

Swoop could not see much around him with the dead man's chest on his face and atop him. He tried to squirm out from under the dead man. He caught glimpses of the other four men as they did the best they could to gather up their senses. But more arrows cut through the campground air. Then a few gunshots.

Some men yelled out in agony.

Indian war whoops.

Then quiet.

It was obvious the five men who trapped him, were down and moaning or dead.

He heard a band of Indians scamper in, talking in a language he was somewhat unfamiliar with, but he understood just a few words. Then, the dead Sugar Bowl Thomas was pulled right off of him, and an Indian stood over him, holding a tomahawk. He glared down at Swoop with a monster's face, painted and wild. The Indian turned Swoop over, face down, and tugged on the wrist ropes. He shouted something after seeing he was bound by the wrists. Then something hit him on the head. Once. Was it the tomahawk? Was he a dead man too? Then came the second blow. It took two hits and Swoop blacked out.

Chapter 3: Corpses, Vultures and Lizards, the Food

Something bit his naked ankle. It woke him up. He rolled over and sat up. He saw an angry, growling coyote near his feet. He saw about 6 coyotes pawing over and biting on the five men lying dead scattered around him.

"AHHHHH! Go! Geet!" Swoop shouted, swatting the one nearest him. He discovered his hands were free!

It winced and backed away. Despite Swoop's pain and injuries and weakness, he got up on a knee and then stood. His hands and ankles were free! He swung wild fists and kicked at the coyote. It growled and howled. He growled and barked back, a lingo these wild dogs understood.

Swoop looked around for a weapon. He dashed over to the cold campfire and grabbed a stick, and with his own growling-yelling plus stick-swinging at them, the pack of coyotes backed off. He looked at his ankle where the animal had nipped him. Minor scratches. He was barefoot!

"Geeet!" he yelled again, waving the stick in the air.

The creatures retreated further away.

"Go on y'all, get! Geeet!"

They did jog off. He tried to remember what happened to him, where he was. The Wells Fargo agents! The Indian attack. He grabbed the top of his head and he still had hair. No scalping. But his hair was matted with blood, and it really hurt with the touch.

He scanned the 5 agents on the ground, and they were not scalped either. Swoop knew well many Indians did not scalp, but some did from either tradition, or they saw the "white man" do it.

Swoop was bootless, and shirtless. They stole his jacket, flannel shirt and boots and they obviously had to cut his wrist and ankle bonds to do so. The agents obviously first took his knife, two Thunderer pistols and tooled belt when they disarmed him and now these weapons were still gone by way of the Indian raid. Stolen twice. Surely those Indians seized them. He had only his torn pants on, and they were ripped and torn in places probably from being tossed from his shot horse. He peeled back the tears to see dried bloody wounds on his legs from a tough landing on the rocks. He shook his head.

He heard something above. He looked up and vultures circled overhead.

He groaned and limped over to the bodies. The other five agents were stripped of their outer clothes also and were almost naked on the ground, left in their underwear.

There were even signs of some torture on one of them. All the horses were gone, stolen. Not a lick of any gear to be found. He took a good look around. Maybe they left his dead horse alone, back there, but where was that? Surely the Indians would strip the carcass of all its tack, maybe even take the body depending upon how hungry they were.

The coyotes and vultures would be eating on that horse too. Maybe even a few buzzards. Swoop knew the difference between vultures and buzzards and how buzzards would eat the dead at times but were more hunters of live prey.

How far had the agents gone from his horse's downfall to set up this camp? Usually at least far enough away to avoid the rotting smells. There would surely be tracks. And his money! Damn! The Indians now had his $200 life savings! His clothes, knife and guns. Hat. Everything. They stole everything that he had and everything else from his Wells Fargo pursuers also. He could tell they even recovered the arrows from the bodies. Such were the ways of roving hunting parties and bands. He could only assume that since he was a bound prisoner of the agents, they let him live? He'd seen this before, let the captured whites live as they must have been enemies and therefore to some extent, comrades. But to what end? Half-naked without food, water, and gear in a desert of canyons. Still, he realized he was so lucky to be alive!

The sun and shadows suggested it was late afternoon. He recalled the men making breakfast. The smell. So, he'd been unconscious for quite a while. The tomahawk! That monster face. He remembered being hit by the toma-hawk, but obviously a flat hammer head side of one, not the sharp side because he would surely otherwise be dead.

There was a steady cool drift of wind. He pulled a torn, bloody thermal undershirt from one corpse and put in on. The others were bare chested.

From his many Army skirmishes with Indians and searches of post battlefield areas both big and small, Swoop knew to inspect the greater area of the fight. Arrows that missed flew afar. The construction of arrows usually led to the identification of tribes, so arrow recovery from raids and battlefields was important. In particular, he considered the range of an arrow, the range of ones that might have missed the agents and might be neglected. He assumed from his memory that the raiding party attack invaded largely from the south. So, he stepped off to the north looking for…arrows.

Once on the move, and somewhat calmed down from chasing off the coyotes (and they would be back), he immediately took note of his aches and pains, which were many from head to toe. After all, he'd been launched off a moving horse! His bare feet stung from the small rocks which meant tough travels ahead.

He calculated the missed arrow distance and made for those potential ranges. And…after a few minutes, there was one on the ground. He studied it. The stone arrowhead and the shaft were fairly sophisticated. The feathers were typical of the birds of Oregon and Utah. And another 20 feet to the left, he found yet another arrow. No more could be spotted, but he now had two arrows. The raiding party had not bothered to fully search and recover a few misses, just the ones that had landed into flesh and bone. Perhaps they didn't care about lost arrows?

When he got back to the campsite, he was suddenly exhausted, but knew he had to keep moving and working. He removed the abandoned underwear from the other four men. Using the tip of an arrow, he made some punctures in one pair, from which he tore 6 crude strips of cloth. He wrapped his feet in two other pairs of underwear and tied the wrappings off with the strips and fashioned some makeshift socks to withstand the apparent long walk ahead to somewhere, anywhere.

On his knees, he examined the extinguished campfire, using a stick to poke and prod the ashes.

"Saints be praised," the part Irishman said, plucking out not one but two long strips of bacon.

He blew on them and slapped the ash off as best he could and ate the bacon, all the while imaging how the Indians yanked the frying pan from the fire, as well as stealing all the cups, pots, pans and silverware the agents surely had. Not a lick of which was left.

The dry, desert-like ground around him was sandy and rocky in spots, with tall and short, thin and wide mesas. Flatlands, rocky desert, mesas, scrub brush and some patches of trees. All the nearby land had the look of the Big Bend, Texas where he'd once been stationed as well as the Garden of the Gods area in Colorado, where he'd recently worked and "hid out" and escaped from the Army bounty hunters.

Swoop stood tall, craning his neck and scrutinized all the surrounding tracks. The Indian ponies were unshod, "barefoot." The horses of the Wells Fargo men had shoes and Swoop decided to follow them back aways. Perhaps he might find his dead horse and it might supply some meat and…blood. Those desperate enough - him - could slit a vein in the horse's neck and drink some blood. A dead horse would have no heartbeat, no blood pressure and the blood would have to be sucked or drawn out. Such measures were taught in cavalry school. Swoop also learned in the Army war college that the Mongols of Asia often preferred to ride lactating horses so they could garnish some milk in the field, and they might even mix the milk with some blood.

It only took about 15 minutes to find a scramble of shod and unshod tracks. Their mix told the story. His horse was left for dead by the agents as his unconscious self was hauled away to the suitable campsite. But such an abandoned horse was a nutritious treasure for hungry Indians and as he feared, his dead horse was gone. On the ground, he could detect the tracks of and presence of a travois, a 'trailer' of sorts, made of long poles and a bed to tow people or objects, or in this case a dead horse off. If the load was heavy and large, one or two other Indians could add their rope and horse to the structure and help pull the travois. He could see where a heavy bed of travois was dragged along the sand and rocks. His horse was gone. The vultures would be landing atop the dead agents soon. They were birds, and birds could be trapped and eaten, but Swoop knew from reading the U.S. military reports about the vulture-germ-bug theory. Vultures were disgusting creatures and carriers of "death germs." Many Indians knew this too and avoided catching and eating them. Just touching them could cause sickness and even death. So, Swoop ruled out trying to touch, catch and eat any vultures.

The sun was setting and there Swoop stood, alone, hungry and lost, in the bloody underwear of dead men with two arrows, one sticking up from each side pocket of his ragged pants. The coyotes would return. The vultures would drop. The flies had already landed. The ants would invade. And he heard wolves howling.

Swoop recollected the image of his lost canyon map in his mind, and he had a working idea of where the Owyhee River ran, which was a bit north from where he figured he was, and the only water he knew of. He would have to head there.

As he took to the nearby higher ground, he kept a close eye out for prickly pear cactus. He knew from his time in the cavalry that he could squeeze the small pink fruit for some drops and then eat the fruit and even the leaves. Many cactus leaves can be cut or broken open and the goo that oozed from inside can be applied to burns, to include sunburn - which he probably would need being stuck out in Owyhee sunlight. The cactus might be rare this far north, but it was known to grow as far up as Idaho according to some Indians he knew. He would also scan the rocks and crevices for bits of dinner "meat" - which would have to be lizards or snakes.

He spied three small lizards and with an arrow he stabbed them. Then he pulled up some of the brush and tree branches along the way for a fire. In an indentation of rocks, almost a cave, he set about the tedious process of starting a fire versus the cold night ahead. He selected a somewhat broad branch and with the arrowhead dug a small depression in it. He put some of the thinnest brush and some bark in it and near it. He stripped a long thin branch, about 2 feet long, and per army instruction, turned it into a spindle. Next came the hard work. He spun the long stick with its point in the depression cut into the wider piece flat on the ground. He remembered from his boot camp training to run his hands up and down the spindle. He'd only done this a few times, learning the trick some 24 years earlier at cavalry school, Ft Sill, Oklahoma and never tried again, as he was always prepared with matches and or flint handy.

The palm-spinning was tiresome, but the wood, grass and bark was dry, and he finally spotted a glowing ember. He quickly spread it to the grass, then some bark, then wood strips. Then he had a fire. He used the arrow to slice open the lizards. He put each on the spindle stick, over the fire, and ate the pathetic little meal.

He heard wolves howling again in the distance as he laid on the rock, half circling the fire, his arrows at hand as lame, mini-spears in case any of nature's monsters, man or beast, should suddenly appear at his caveman home.

Sunrise. Cold. Very cold. The fire was out, and he felt as though he was frozen to the ground. He dreamed of the coming eastern sun, the warm sun of the afternoon beating down on him. Oh, what a great feeling that would be. Then that would turn horrible again when it vanished west.

He slowly moved, painfully, and sat up. Time to head north, as simply based on the sunrise and sunset directions. Within a few hours, Swoop came to an open, rather flat field of sporadic grasses. Upon it were maybe a hundred or more white-gray mounds in the distance.

As he got closer, as he had expected, he identified that these mounds where the torso bones of long dead rotted buffaloes. It was a haunting, hunted graveyard. He examined the remains as he drew near. These creatures were shot for sure and skinned on site, maybe years ago. The bleached bones were long picked clean of any meat or organs. The mounds were spaced out for butchering. Swoop calculated this carnage was performed many years ago.

When walking in amongst them, he knew there were well more than one hundred. Swoop knew abandoned bones like these were worth something to businesses. Bison bones were collected and processed in middle America and the East for glue, fertilizer, dyes, and even burned to create a "bone char," a component in sugar refining. And here, like so many buffalo graveyards they rotted away, the hunters seeking only the skins and maybe some organs and tongues.

The cavalry and many westerners and western-bound folks were used to burning buffalo dung or "chips" when wood was scarce. The chips burned surprisingly well and produced an odor-free flame, but judging from the age of this site, those chips were long gone.

Otherwise, a close scrutiny of each set of bones, or locating the campsite of the hunters might turn up discarded tools and abandoned gear. No matter how long ago this site was once a live butcher shop. Swoop was near exhaustion. How long dare he linger to maybe find a dull, rusty knife or an old coffee cup? He needed to march on to his dream of finding the river.

There was nothing salvageable for him to use. He trudged on, wondering if in his current predicament, he would end in a little mound of his own ribs somewhere like these. A searcher of his bones in the future would find two arrowheads in his tattered pants pockets.

Chapter 4: Sagiswatch, the Indian

Each day grew worse. More hunger. More thirst. More fatigue. More heat in the day. More cold at night. He did find some prickly pear cacti and recovered some drops of water. His face was sunburnt, and he cut the leaves with an arrowhead and rubbed some of the leaf goo on his face and cheeks, as well as on some of his cuts, which he did not know would actually help. With his arrows he speared and ate a snake and a few more lizards.

Shivering, he slept on the rocks and hard ground the fourth night…

…he was asleep in a bed, in the dark, in a strange place. Then he felt the side of the bed drop down, like someone had slipped in it. Who? He tried to turn to see who or what it was. He could only move his head, not his body. It was a ghostly, ethereal of a blueish-gray woman, laughing like a monster. But it was his dead wife! Half rotted. He yelled-screamed…

And he woke up on the tough soil, gasping. He opened his eyes to see something else startling, what he thought might have been another mirage-dream, a hallucination at first, but it wasn't. There before the orange sunrise was a man, squatting, watching him from about ten feet away.

"You screamed out. Ha!" the man said, "The spirits in your head know how to warn you that there is danger near when you sleep. So, they give you a nightmare to make you wake up."

Swoop said nothing. He sat up and took a good look at him. The man was obviously an Indian, about 50 years old, very thin, in boots, long pants, a plaid shirt under a dark blue jacket, and a top hat with feathers. He held no weapon.

"I speak white," the man said. "Who are you?"

"A lost man."

"How did you get here, lost man?"

"Indians raided my group. They left me alive."

"Who Indians?"

"I don't know."

"Why?"

"I don't know. You have food? Water?" Swoop asked.

"Yes," the Indian said but he did not move.

Groggy, Swoop looked around for a horse. None he could see.

"I should kill you," the Indian said.

"Kill…why?" Swoop said.

"Because, to finish the work of my brothers."

"They did not kill me for a reason," Swoop said.

The Indian grunted and said, "What reason?"

"I don't know."

They stared at each other.

"My name is Sagiswatch. I am mostly Wasco. Mostly. I travel among all."

"I know some Chinook," Swoop said, knowing that main tribal language was much the basis for numerous, regional Indian dialects. "Do you have any food or water?" Swoop had to ask again.

"How you know Chinook?"

"I am a prospector. Gold. I travel too. I've been to many places. Do you have any food or water?"

The Indian stood and then walked completely around and behind Swoop. His horse was standing quietly directly behind Swoop. Swoop, still seated on the ground, swung around on his rear end to watch him, worried that the Indian might pull a pistol or rifle. Instead, the man produced a canteen and a handful of beef jerky.

"I still should kill you," he said again, "but it might be the wishes of my brothers to keep you alive. Why they do not kill you?"

"I don't know, they only hit me in the head, but they killed five other men with me. They stole everything from us."

Swoop took the canteen knowing not to gorge himself. He sipped. He took the little pile of jerky, biting down on one piece with an explosion of flavor on his virgin tongue.

Sagiswatch backed away, leaving the food and canteen with Swoop.

"You have two Paiute arrows in your pockets. How come?"

"These are the only two arrows the raiders missed killing my friends with. I found the arrows on the ground."

"Hmmm. Smart to look for. How you know such tricks?"

"Desperate," Swoop said.

"You army?"

"No."

"Hmmm. One time Army?"

"No."

"Hmmm."

Sip. Sip. Sip. Sip in silence.

"I should still kill you. But I will follow the wishes of my brothers."

Sip. Sip. Then Sagiswatch reached out and snatched the canteen.

"But instead, I will leave you as my brothers wished. How they did, here. In your underwear. But I need a payment from you. A trade for my food and water. They took your boots, eh?"

"Yes."

"Your boots were a payment to let you live. I think."

"They took my hat, jacket, shirt and boots. My guns and knife. Everything from everyone else too and still killed them. I don't know about such payments. But they are dead. And I am here without food or water. Or boots," Swoop said.

"This is boring to me. I will take my payment now too for the jerk and water you ate and drank. But, you have nothing to pay me with. So, you will pay me with - as you white people say- a 'tattoo,' on your body because you have nothing to trade me for your memory of our meeting, of the food and water I give you. Payment. So, a nice cut on you is payment. A scar!"

Sagiswatch pulled out a knife and rushed him! He dashed suddenly, racing in on Swoop, both arms up and ready for a grab and a cut. Once so exhausted, Swoop still flew into a rage of power. He stood up in time to hit both Sagiswatch's arms outward with his forearms, braced a leg back and punched the Indian in the face. Once, twice, three fists in two seconds like the war college boxer he once was. Sagiswatch tumbled backward, dropped the knife and fell on his rear, his top hat flying way off his head.

Swoop, breathless, stood before him. He pulled an arrow from his pocket to stab with, ready for more.

"*Aipui*!" Sagiswatch yelled out, but to whom?

Swoop recognized the Chinook or Shoshone word for "destroy," but it was too late. Sagiswatch's horse obeyed the order and was next to charge at him from behind. The trained horse knew the translation too well. The steed ran right into Swoop as Swoop barely started to turn to the sound of its hooves. He began a dodging leap aside when the horse rammed him almost full on. And like a week before, Swoop once again flew through the air from a horse, then crashed down on the flat rocks with the horse still in pursuit but trying not to trip over him. It did stomp down on him somewhat.

Angry, hurt again, Swoop crawled away from the horse and its owner, trying to stand, but couldn't.

"There! There is your tattoo from my horse, you crazy fool hobo. Your payment! Your memory," Sagiswatch declared as he got to his feet.

"I'm crazy?" Swoop said, "who helps a starving man and then wants to cut him!"

"I should just kill you, hobo! But your slower death out here as a hobo of the desert and canyon is better for your end."

The horse snorted, and now stood beside the man. He picked up his canteen, his hat and knife and mounted the horse. He was bleeding from his nose and mouth. He too snorted like his horse and wiped the blood on the sleeve of his jacket.

"You will die out here, desert and canyon hobo. Good for you, crazy fool."

Swoop sat still, more or less, on the ground where the horse's charge left him. Sagiswatch rode off to the south.

Then, Swoop half crawled back over to the scattered

pile of beef jerky and ate some of it, saving some for later. He stood slowly, testing his right leg as it really hurt. It was not broken. He picked up the arrow he dropped when hit by the horse and limped north, hunting for more prickly pear cacti, snakes and lizards and the river.

Where was that river?

What was the name, if there is a river?

He couldn't think straight.

Chapter 5: Father Penance, the Savior
Day six. Sunset...

Swoop, dizzy and famished, had lost most of his appetite
at this point, which he knew was dangerous. The cactus,
the snakes and lizards, however meager, probably kept
him barely alive. He climbed and crawled atop a small
mesa for a look around. He had to lay on his chest to examine the landscape as he was that exhausted. Vultures
were still following him, circling high overhead for days.

The river! Finally! And what? Light! Fires! He spotted
a compound, something shaped like a southwestern fort
with small buildings within it, just on the far side of the
river. If this was an Army fort, he could be captured. But
captured and alive for a while longer or die of exposure
and starvation tonight or tomorrow.

"That a...church?" Swoop whispered, hoping it was
not another mirage as he'd started to see many things,
many shapes, and many nightmares he confused with re-
ality.

He rubbed his eyes and squinted to see more. The

campfires lit up the area. It was indeed a large, walled compound. Several buildings. And…yes…a church with a steeple on the front east end side. Old. Very old looking, much like the ones he'd seen in New Mexico and Arizona.

Torches lit the front doors and several fires burned inside the walls. There was a wide dirt road in front of the church, a river road as far as he could see to the right and left, running east and west. The compound looked to be about 200 yards away. Forty yards down this hill, about 100 yards to the river, 40 yards across the river and the rest to the church doors.

"Civil…civilization at last," Swoop mumbled, "but the river. Can I make it down to it and across that river?"

The Owyhee River was quite wide, but maybe not too deep. The red reflections of the door torches rippling on the current revealed a fairly fast-moving waterway. It would be no problem for a well-rested, well-fed Swoop Swellen to get across that river, but Swoop felt like he was almost dead. Could he even get to the river's edge, least of all cross it?

"Okay. Get up Swellen," he ordered himself, "You've lasted this long. You've got to last. Last. Last."

He rose up onto his sore and cut feet. He crossed the rest of the short mesa top. The far side was not too steep, and he started to descend. Rocks and dirt turned loose and dribbled down ahead of him. One of his makeshift, now very torn, shoe-sock-wraps peeled off of a foot, but he did not stop his decent.

Then he fell, stumbling from unsure footing or just sheer exhaustion, or both. Yet another headfirst plunge, with the same feeling as when his shot horse died under him last week and when Sagiswatch's horse rammed him. He was pitched airborne yet again.

He slid to a stop about 20 feet down. Upside down, face down, he groaned and spit out the dirt. He crawled down the rest of the side, came to somewhat level land.

And though he could barely stand, he did.

"Last," he said. "Last."

The river was ahead. Just ahead. And beyond the waterway he saw a man walk out the front doors of the church.

"Hey! HEEEEY" he yelled out, surprised how feeble and scratchy his voice sounded. The man apparently could not hear him.

"Hey!"

He started to run as best he could like a very bad, unbalanced drunk, to the river, with each step spike like stones into his tender, cut and cracked feet.

"He…ahhh…hey! Hey…"

Dizzy again, he quickly started panting. He got near the river's side and the man by the church was gone. But that church and compound was very real. He knew it. He smelled the smoke from the fires.

The water was moving fast. He laid chest down and wormed his way to hang his face over the river. He drank. The water was shockingly cold. He stuck as much of his head in as possible.

"Last," he said again. "Last"

Then he sat up, cross-legged and thought about crossing the river and reaching the church's big, open, double doors. He thought it a good idea to twist around and stick his ravaged feet in the cold water first. He did. It felt good and then bad. It made him dizzy. Then good.

"Can I make this?" he asked himself, hypnotized by the fires' red reflections on the moving water.

"Come on Swellen, you can last that long…last…"
But instead, he passed out, his numb feet still in the water.

Morning…
Father Federico Penance was a 60-year-old priest with the Roman Catholic Church. He was once headquartered in Juarez, Mexico. Penance was half Spanish, half French,

he could speak both languages as well as English. Some might say down South that he was banished to the high canyons way up north from his past misdeeds and hidden away from the mainstream church's reach and normal people and business.

He thought little of himself anymore, ashamed of his past, his trials and tribulations, all of which made him a blackmailed prisoner to this obscure church and its odd orphanage. He'd long ago lost his belief in God, yet he donned his black robes every day. He mindlessly did his religious chores and said mass every Sunday because…because he had to. Those around him made him, even threatened him to do so. They counted on him. He wanted to believe again, to believe in things, just couldn't anymore. Too unfaithful for faith. He just wanted to leave, but he couldn't. Where would he go? He was in a sense a prisoner of the church, its accomplices and it's so-called "orphanage."

After his morning coffee and bread, he and Mel Svenson opened the two giant, weathered front doors of the 80-year old church as if an invitation for anyone interested to come walking in. They could, but they would be met by an armed guard.

There was only a very busy, very small congregation of ranchers and some farmers in this remote area that bothered to walk in. Once in a while. Holidays.

The river road was busy once in a while, as busy as the old Oregon Trail itself. The road had some travelers afoot, on horseback and even the occasional wagon train. They all stopped in as a respite from their trips. Father Penance greeted them and said his routine empty prayers over them.

With him was Mel Svenson from Sweden. He was dressed in the modern white shirt, black jacket and pants of a clergyman. He was not one. He was introduced to visitors and orphans as a deacon. He was not. It was Svenson's job to guard the front door wearing a pistol and brandishing a rifle, prepared to fend off the untrustworthy looking, the robbers, thieves and the occasional renegade Indians that might attack.

They pulled open one side of the double doors. Svenson and Father Penance surveyed the surroundings after opening the second door, as was their habit. The father's scan was not a shallow one.

"Is that…what is that?" Father Penance said. "Over there."

"What?"

"That thing over there. Across the river. Is that…is that a man laying down over there?"

Mel Svenson craned his neck to see. There was indeed something light-colored on the dark tan and almost red ground.

"I think it's a man," Father Penance said.

"He spying on us?" Svenson said. "He got a rifle? Telescope?"

"No, I…I think he's dead. Come on."

"I don't like it."

"I don't like it either, but I think it's a dead man," the priest said, "come on."

"Veve better find out vat killed him. Maybe the damn Utes?" Svenson said. "Ve can't be having them back attacking us again."

The two walked to the river's edge. Svenson peeled off his black shoes and pants and dropped them on the ground, but the Father didn't remove his full robes and sandals. Then they waded into the water, with Svenson cursing in Swedish over the cold. At the deepest parts, it only came up to their waistline. Svenson held the rifle high and pulled the pistol from the holster. Still the medium water flow made the trek difficult. The closer they got the worse it looked for the prone figure.

"You see, he is not a spy and there's no rifle or telescope," Father Penance declared.

When the men got closer in, they started calling out to him.

"Hey! You! Mister! You there!"

When closest, Father Penance kneeled down beside him.

"Sir! Sir. Are you still with us? Hola!"

"He's dead as a rock," Svenson said, while leaning over and slapping Swoop's face. Nothing. "Look at that bloody shirt."

"The blood is very dry," Father Penance said as he pulled the man's feet out of the water. They were white and bloated.

"Well, his feet are like ice bergs. And look at the cuts on them," he said as he then clasped his hands before him, still on his knees.

Father Penance closed his eyes, lowered his head, and reflexively began the prayer of death's passage. "Through this holy anointing may the Lord in his love and mercy help you with the grace of the Holy Spirit. May the Lord who frees you from sin save you and raise you up. May you…"

"May…may, I have some water. Holy water will do," Swoop suddenly said in a low rasp.

Both men were startled. Svenson even stumbled backwards.

"Mister, what happened," the priest asked.

"Indians. Attacked us. My friends are dead. I escaped," Swoop said in a parched whisper.

Svenson immediately scanned the area for these Indians. Bringing the rifle up to aim across the mesa.

"Miles away. Many. I escaped."

"They follow you?" Svenson asked.

"I don't think so," Swoop said, a bit aghast even at his exhausted state watching a half-naked man of the cloth brandishing a rifle.

"Is anything broken?" Father Penance asked.

"Not that I can remember," Swoop said, "maybe now though? I just fell. Fell back there."

"Let us see. What is your name, sir?" the priest asked.

"Ahhh…Last. Charles…Last," Swoop lied again.

"Well, you lasted this long, Mr. Last," the priest said and slowly helped Swoop sit up. "I am Father Penance of the Lord's High Desert Parish. You are not the first wretched soul from the desert canyons to come to our little church."

"Yeah," Swoop grunted, as the priest squatted to reach under his arm and shoulder.

He started to stand and Svenson got a grip under the other shoulder.

"Let us cross the river," Penance said.

"Let us," Swoop whispered, noting now how his voice was so desiccated it burned to speak. "Water though. Water. Even holy water."

"Yes, yes we will get you some water and food," Penance said. "It won't be holy water because water is just water, no matter how many words you pray over it."

This pronouncement annoyed Svenson, who sneered at Penance.

The three traversed the river and made it to the other side. With each step Swoop was losing consciousness. Once at the doors, he lost it.

Chapter 6: Sister Rosalinda, the Nun

Swoop awoke to a strange world. He was naked on a bed inside a small adobe room with one small, closed slatted-shutter window. The sun beamed in through the chipped away and worn slats. Of all things, he also awoke with a nun seated right beside him, her hand stroking his bare belly.

"Ahhh, is this some kind of strange Heaven?" Swoop said with a dry gasp that hurt his throat. He coughed.

He looked down at himself. Some effort was made to clean up and cover his wounds, but he was still caked in some mud and dirt. He felt of his face. He was clean shaven with the beginnings of a moustache.

"There, there, now," the nun said. "Do you like your

moustache? I like your moustache."

As his eyes came into focus, he looked at her. All he could see of her was her face under the winged hat and bulky robes of a nun. She appeared to be in her 40s with a touch of makeup on - which would be unique to the order, Swoop thought.

"I am Sister Rosalinda. You can call me Rosy… when…you know, we are alone."

Her palm ran up his torso and the hand flipped over for the stroke back down.

"Rose…Sister Rosalinda," Swoop said.

"Yeah."

"Where am I?"

"You are in the Lord's High Canyon Parish. A bedroom off the church hallway. We have many rooms here. We are also an orphanage. An orphanage for lost and wayward children."

"Uh-huh. The Lord's…yeah…"

"Are you a wayward…man?" She asked coyly.

"Hmmm, ah. I don't know. Some would say."

"We will…straighten you out then. Oh my, I see now that you are beginning to straighten…"

Then the room door suddenly opened and two men walked in. One was Father Penance. Sister Rosalinda quickly removed her hand from Swoop's body, but the swift removal was observed by both visitors.

"How is our guest, Sister," the stranger with the Father asked, smirking at the nun for what he knew she must have been doing.

"He has just…awakened, Deacon," she said.

She stood, grimaced, and with a slight nod to both, she left the room.

"I am Deacon Ambrose, Mr. Last," the stranger said. "I run this place. The working manager. Father Penance is the high ordained priest here, but I manage all the…I ramrod the workings around here."

Swoop struggled to sit up a bit. Father Ambrose was about 40 years old. Black curly hair. Chubby. Unshaven. His nose hairs were so thick it looked like they could fall down and start a moustache. Immediately, Swoop could smell the mix of alcohol he emitted from his breath and his stained white shirt. There was also a stench of urine about him.

"Father Penance said that you were attacked by an Indian party."

Swoop looked at the priest, his first good, straight-on, look. He'd been too near dead earlier, to memorize any features. Penance had the long nose, dark skin, and the look of some of the South Americans he'd met in Baton Rouge, LA. He was a little man, especially standing next to Ambrose.

"Ahh yes, there were five of us on our way to Seattle and, and we were bushwhacked. We were all left for dead. The others died and I didn't. I had a map of the area in my mind and had an idea of where the river was."

"What was your purpose for coming this way?" Deacon Ambrose asked.

"Ahh, prospecting."

"Yes. Yes, we get a lot of hopeful prospectors pass by here and stop in for blessings. We have the neighboring Northern Paiute, Bannock and Shoshone tribes around here. Nez Piercers. Friendly, well, sometimes friendly. Usually. But then there are groups within them, not at all friendly. Committing outrages and depredations. We also try to convert those that we can into our Christianity."

"Uh-huh," Swoop said, still half dazed and trying to concentrate on the deacon's words.

"Our little church and orphanage here have been attacked by them at times, but we are like a fort here. Smartly done by our predecessors. God's little fort. And we held to our mission, held our mission's ground."

"Uh-huh. I saw that one of you was armed."

"Yes. We must stay armed and alert, and at the same time keep our front doors open. People living here and people passing by, often dropping in and…dropping off children. The poor children of traveling parents murdered and…or killed by accidents. Did you know how many accidents there are on wagon trains?"

"I heard many."

Father Penance stood by in silence, but grabbed a wooden cup of water nearby and handed it to Swoop. Swoop sipped it.

"More people are killed by cattle and traveling accidents than anything else. Well, their children suddenly have no parents, and the traveling companions see only strife ahead, so they leave them here with us, hoping for a stable adoption. We…we arrange such things. Some also drop their teenage troublemakers off too, so we have some discipline problems also. We teach them the lessons of Christ."

"Un-huh," Swoop said, fighting off falling back to sleep. Each heavy-lidded, blink of his eyes, might bring instant sleep.

"You are in good hands, Mr. Last. Hands of the Lord. We will help you recover. Get up on your feet. Perhaps you might join a wagon train passing by and continue your life?"

"Thanks. Y'all saved my life."

"Sister Rosalinda will see to you. Don't mind her ways. She is like a chameleon, like a child or a teenager herself. We are all trying to survive our obscure ordained life out here. She will arrange a hot bath to chisel off the rest of the canyon muck clinging to you still, and she will get you some clothes. All we have in your adult sizes are religious vestments of deacons in black. Good day to you sir. Rest."

"Vestments…" Swoop mumbled.

They left. Swoop collapsed fully back on the bed.

Sister Rosalinda walked back in. She grinned.

"Now Charles, where were we?"

Ambrose and Penance walked down the side hall of the church.

"Svenson tells me you made some unholy comments about holy water when bringing this man in across the river," Ambrose said.

"Well, I…" Penance started.

Ambrose stopped. Penance had to stop too.

"Remember Freddy, you need to keep your heathen mouth shut. We need to have an image around here to maintain our business. I know you still have some religion left in you. Svenson told me you started to give the man his last rites."

"I did. I did so. Like a reflex." The Father said.

"Well, you keep those old reflexes alive, Freddy. Keep them coming," Ambrose said. "Do not go atheist on me, you hear? There's too much money involved."

"Yes, sir."

"We'll patch up this Charles Last and ship him off quickly. He'll speak well of us if we do. Ask him to write a letter to the Bishop in Juarez."

They parted ways at the end of the hall with Father Penance turning the corner and off for his primitive office in the back of the church, which he secretly referred to as his prison cell.

Chapter 7: Nerto, the Renegade Chief

Near a grove of trees by a small stream in a narrow canyon, in among the short ranges of hills and mesas these canyonlands offered, Sagiswatch spotted some Indians and their camp. The wide crevasse offered cool shade from the sun, as well as a breeze he could feel from far away. He counted 24 men, two of which were standing guard atop both small peaks on either side of the canyon.

"One, two, three," he counted aloud…He saw 30 horses and observed some of the men in western wear clothing, as he himself was dressed. He assumed this was the raiding party that left this wandering white canyon-hobo man alive.

He approached with some caution. One never knew what one's reception might bring within tribe to tribe, and nation to nation. New grudges and hostilities could have broken out that such a traveling, isolated Sagiswatch might not have known of, or little did he know about some war parties that break from their traditions and run amok. He did know about the troublesome Nerto though, and his accomplices. Nerto was not a chief, not even an elder, but a thirty-year old Indian was of some consequence, and somewhat popular. He and his men were known to raid and bring some occasional riches back to their Ute tribes.

The elders, trying to keep the U.S. Cavalry off their backs, and dealing with a new U.S. Government appointed chief that frowned at such raids and deliveries.

Within a minute the ridge top guards spotted Nerto and recognized him from a distance by the top hat.

"Sagiswatch come in," one guard shouted down to their leader.

Nerto grunted at the news. Sagiswatch was the roaming bearer of gossip though and someone to remain friendly with because of his neutral connections.

"Alone?" Nerto said.

"Yes."

"Okay then."

Sagiswatch casually rode in, nodding and waving to some. Some returned the greeting, some did not. He spotted Nerto and dismounted.

"*Behne!*" Sagaswatch said, walking up to Nerto. He sat down on one of the big blankets around the leader.

"*Behne*," Nerto replied.

"I have some English tea with me. You want a drink. We have to make hot water," Sagiswatch said.

"Yes. I am tired of their coffee. Tea, yes," Nerto said, and he told a man by a food fire to boil some water.

They spoke of Sagiswatch's travels, Nerto of his. He mentioned the recent raid.

"So why did you let that one white man live?" Sagiswatch asked.

"That white man? He was a prisoner of the other white men. Wollow wanted his shirt. Nice shirt that the mountain lumberjacks wear. Many colored lines up and down And side to side. Wollow!"

Wollow walked over to them in his new shirt.

"Very nice. They call it flannel," Sagiswatch said of the modeling. Wollow stroked his sleeves with his hands. And raised his eyebrows at the quality.

"We took many shirts, but many have arrow and bullet holes because we had to kill the fools," Wollow said. "This one? No. No holes."

"So, he cut the bounds of the prisoner," Nerto said,
"Bounds?"

"Yes, to get the shirt. Wollow took his shirt. We did not kill this prisoner."

"He was their prisoner?"

"Yes. We think that maybe he is an enemy of the other white men. They had him tied up. And then we are some kind of brother to him."

"You leave him to die?"

"Eh. He is on his own," Nerto said. "What happens, happens."

"Who was with him, then?"

Nerto leaned far over, almost toppling over, to reach a leather satchel and pulled it to him. He opened the drawstring at the top.

"Look. Five of them were Wells Fargo. Look," Nerto said as he pulled five badges from the satchel and displayed them over his two open hands.

"Ohhhh! Five badges. This is really something," Sagis-watch said. "They are lawmen. And what is this you wear? Your guns?"

"Yes," Nerto said and sat up straight. "Two pistol gun belt. Two nice pistols. Same kind each. Nice knife."

"Let me see one."

Nerto pulled a pistol and handed it to Sagiswatch.

"This is a very nice gun. Thunderer. Thunderer, you see. It says on the side."

"I do not read white. I like that name though," Nerto said, "Thunderer. Very nice. I like this. Like Senawahv, the God of lightning and thunder too, eh?"

"Like Senawahv. It is a sign to get these, yes. Look at the belt to keep the pants up. Nice. Yes," Nerto said and smiled.

"The white's call this a dress belt or a pants belt," Sagiswatch said.

"The gun belt was laying on a saddle. The pants belt was from that same white man that you speak of. We let the white man live. But…anyway, I left him to die slowly in the canyon lands if he had bad luck."

"I see, but he is still alive."

"He is?"

"I saw him four days ago. He begs me for food and water, and I gave him some. But when I want my price, my payment in return for my gifts. He has nothing. No trade."

Nerto nodded.

"You know, I think, maybe I leave a scar on him or take a tooth. I moved in to leave a mark and the devil punched me down on my ass. My nose!" he touched it, "he made it bleed and go flat."

"Around your eyes are black. You know this?"

"No. But it hurts all around there," he said, pressing his fingertips around his eyes. I called for my horse to ram him down. He did, knocking the man flying. Then, that was my price. I left him."

"*Jahabich*!" Nerto declared.

"I left him because I did not know the reason you left him. Maybe a good one? Strange man. But, now very weak. Almost dead, but still, he sprang up to punch me down with the speed and strength of a teenage warrior. What else you get from the Wells Fargo men? Some money?"

"Yes. 216 dollars."

"This is great money."

"Then some papers that I cannot read. No one here can."

"I read white. Let me see."

Nerto called for Wollow to get all the dead men's saddlebags.

Wollow came back with the bags. Nerto opened them all and handed him a stack of papers. Nerto started reading them, page by page.

"Yes…yes…they were detectives from Wells Fargo, yes. Yes. They were working to find some lost gold dust in Oregon. Robbers. Yes. They are from St. Louis. And… HA! Ha, Nerto! Did you not see this one?"

"What? No. We cannot read these papers. We did not look at them."

"Look!" He held up a page for Nerto to see.

"You see this paper? This is a wanted paper, a wanted poster the whites call them."

"I know what they call them."

"This man you let live? He was their prisoner. Yes. He is wanted by the Army for $1,000! Nerto! LOOK at this face!"

Nerto took the paper and looked at the drawn face.

"This is the man you let go!" Sagiswatch said. "And this is the man I left alive too. This is the man Wells Fargo held prisoner. Once a general. In their Army. Named

Swellen."

"So?" Nerto said, "The Army hates him. Good. He then is our…"

"So? So? He is wanted dead or alive for $1,000!"

"So what! They will never pay an Indian $1,000!" Nerto said.

"Maybe not youuuu! You are too much Indian. Look at you. But me? I know people. All kinds of people. I could try something, do something to bring him in and get this $1,000. I know the Indian agent at the Umatilla Agency. He is a white man and a good friend of mine. A good man. He is fair. We could turn this Swellen man in to him, dead or alive to him. I trust him to pay us."

"Huh?"

"I go to the Oregon Rendezvous every year. Indians and whites trade. Dance and sing. I make friends with many good whites there. I know I can trust some of them."

"How they pay?"

"Paper money."

"No coins?"

"No, Nerto, $1,000, it's too many coins. Listen to me Nerto, we track this man down. If he is dead, we take the body in. If he is alive, we must capture him and take the man in. Or we kill him. Doesn't matter. Dead or alive. We will split up the $1,000. There is what…almost 30 of us?"

"Yes. Yes, but maybe we give less to these other men. After all, you know, we are their leaders," Nerto said.

"Yeeees," Sagiswatch said, nodding.

"We could buy many things? At such a rendezvous? With this money?"

"OH! Oh, many things. You may have no idea. You could take many helpful things back to the Utes. Food. Drink. Tools. Guns. Clothes. Horses. You should see what they have. Tools and new inventions."

"Take back to them? I don't know. Maybe I will keep. I

don't much like the new Chief Tante Ourai. He is chosen by the whites to be big Chief."

"Oh, I hear he is just okay," Nerto said.

"In the end, no white man choice is good for the Indian."

"I know what you mean," Sagiswatch said with a grimace.

"I think I want to start my own people. My own tribe. Away from the whites. Away from these other Indians who trust the whites."

"I know what you mean. But, you will never get away from the whites. They are like a blanket over everything," Sagiswatch said.

"Hmm! We shall hunt down this general then," Nerto said. "I can use this money to make a small tribe."

"Yes. If he were to survive somewhere, the only place he could go, would be at that Catholic church of the lost children on the river road. When I tracked him, he was going that way."

"We have raided that church before," Nerto said, "and we rescued some Indian children from their Catholic ways. We had a shootout. The place is like a fort, but we got in."

"You have guns now?"

"Yes. We save the bullets and use arrows when we can," Nerto said.

"Good idea. But you can buy many bullets with the bounty."

"You have a gun?" Nerto asked.

"Yes. A pistol," Sagiswatch answered, patting his side.

"Good. Bullets?" Nerto asked.

"A box. Yes."

"Good," Nerto said. "We go into the church if we have to, and we get him from inside there if he's there. And… and, I think we will take all the girls and women too."

"The women are nuns. They hide from sex."

"We rape them. Nuns are good for breeding and work. Tribes always like them. Good for us here. The church has young ones. I want to start my own people, away from Chief Tante Ourai."

Sagiswatch nodded.

"Tonight, tomorrow morning we eat, sleep, then go off and look for the tracks of this man. You must stay the night here with us."

"Yes," Sagiswatch said.

"And we will dream of this $1,000," Nerto said.

"Yes."

Chapter 8: Luke and Janet Gresham, the Twins

Swoop awoke and could smell the scent of breakfast in the air. He'd been nibbling food and sipping goat's milk for 2 days or maybe more, all sustenance that the rambunctious Sister Rosalinda had delivered along with her constant groping and petting. He was not sure what went on with the Sister during his first delirious, hallucinating, feverish hours and days there.

She even insisted on helping him get dressed when he couldn't stand. He was outfitted with used sandals, old black pants too long in the crotch, a used, once white - now mostly light grey shirt and a frayed black jacket with a priest's collar. What he really needed was socks, as the cracked and cut soles of his feet still bled somewhat, and he feared infection. The Sister had been washing them. He had a dream or a nightmare about her singing bawdy bar room songs while scrubbing his feet. How would a nun know those songs?

His bed was a dark, wooden frame, very old and stout, with a soiled mattress filled with loose cloth, or so it felt. His pillow was a rolled-up worn towel. A prickly Navajo blanket was his only cover. But he was alive!

He took a deep breath, stood up from the bed and since there was a chill in the air, put on the lightweight, black suit jacket. He rubbed his face surprised to feel it was clean shaven. Rosy must have struck again while in his feverish sleep.

Then with his first painful steps of the morning, he entered the hallway. The breeze and brightest sunlight came from the left and he walked that way. With a right turn he entered the church they first dragged him through the other day. Two days ago? Three? The front doors were open and a big man in priest's clothing, same as his, sat in a wicker chair just inside the doors, a rifle on his lap.

"Veellll, look who's up," the man said. He had a Nordic accent.

He looked like the big man who had helped him across the river, but wasn't sure, but it sounded like him.

"Yes. Expecting…trouble?" Swoop asked. This was the first good look at the other of his riverside rescuers. He was a classic. Tall, blonde-headed, in his 40s and with that accent.

"Ve need to post a guard here. Ve are ordered to keep the doors of the church open, but ve have been attacked by Indians and some criminals. And ve have travelers coming by sometimes. Most are friendly. Some…unfriendly."

"I see," Swoop said, "I think I smell bacon and coffee. Where's it coming from?"

"That vay, cross the open courtyard. Double doors, go in, then this vay, that vay," he gave the final directions with his hands.

"Thanks," Swoop said.

The interior of the church was the classic Spanish influence he'd seen all over the southwest. Painted adobe walls and a stone-tiled floor. Rows and rows of very pitted, aged pews. Bad wooden, religious statues, looking like they were chopped into their crude forms by a drunk. The ugly effigies surrounded an altar right up front with a big simplistic cross made of two big, local, gnarly tree branches, roped together.

Swoop stepped out onto the big, open walled court-yard. The sun hurt his eyes. Squinting, he saw that it did indeed resemble a fort inside there. Other than some sun-dried, dilapidated furniture and several firepits, the area was mostly empty, except for a garden in a far northwest corner and three water pumps. On the back wall were a number of outhouses. These outhouses seemed vaguely familiar as he must have been carried out to them in the last few days.

He turned to see the church had a back door and he had a flashback of being in an outhouse…with Sister Rosa-linda standing over him, smiling. He shook his head free of the image. Maybe that was a dream? Children in dirty clothes were cleaning the outhouses out. One girl gagged.

The west wall had one long building, the south end of it looked like the orphanage and the north end must have been the mess hall – as a soldier such as he, might call it. The northeast corner had a nicer building. As Swoop limped by it all, it was obvious to him where the staff lived. It resembled what he would identify as the "of-ficer's quarters." In the far northwest corner, there was a barn with stables and a chicken pen just outside the open doors.

The outer walls were about ten feet tall, and some broad wooden boxes were set up for people to stand on and see over the top.

Some kids sat on the hard ground, and some walked around in the garden. Some tended to the chickens. They all looked ragged. They stared at him as though he were a strange animal. Perhaps it was his limp? Swoop smiled at them but then they quickly looked away.

He followed his nose through open double doors and into that "mess hall" like cafeteria. Big inside. Old wooden tables and benches. Big religious, stained-glass windows caught his eye that were quite artistic, unlike the artifacts in the church. No telling how long they'd been displayed there and what they must have survived when one guessed how old this compound was. There were two serving tables of food, and Swoop made his way toward one. He could see bowls of beans, rice and old discolored lettuce, patrolled by flies. The food choices there looked poor…

"No!" Father Penance shouted out, "this one, over there."

Swoop turned for the other table near Penance and it was better stocked. Fruit. Eggs. Bacon. Beans. Coffee. This spread was clearly for the staff while the kids and teens were assigned the lame one. One teenager's job was to fan and swat at the flies with a small pillow tied to a stick. Swoop nodded at the teen, but the kid looked away.

Starving, Swoop filled a plate and got a cup of coffee, he sat near Father Penance, who was alone.

"How are you feeling," Penance asked.

"Better. Way better. I'm sure after this meal I'll be better still. I heard more about how y'all found me. Rescued me from the dead. I couldn't remember everything about it."

"We thought you were dead Mr. Last. I started your last rites you know."

"I was on my last rites," Swoop said in a garble, chewing his breakfast.

After some mouthfuls and gulps of lukewarm coffee he continued, "So I think it is quite the coincidence that a priest is named Penance."

"That is not my real name," the Father said. "My real last name is Santisima. Remedios Cipriano de la Santísima."

"That is a mouthful," Swoop said with a mouthful.

The Bishop in Juarez gave me the last name of Penance to make things harder for everyone. Make me remember. Always be seeking penance, he would say."

"I see."

"And a reminder to me, to remind me that I always need penance. And I have sure done my penance being way out here, way up here."

"The kids, how many do you have?"

"We have 20 children and 16 teenagers up to 16 years old."

"Thirty-six kids. And they only get to eat from that one table?" Swoop asked.

"They do."

"It's some mighty dried-out, slim pickins over there."

"Well, Penance said, "we have decided that the staff here, for our continual health and so forth, must be maintained so we can keep the church and orphanage open."

"How many people work here?"

"Six nuns. Ten men of cloth."

"All the men are priests?" Swoop asked.

"No, they are all…deacons.

"Even Ambrose?"

"Even Ambrose. He is the head deacon. The working manager."

"And deacons are on their way, on the path to becoming priests?"

"They all have yet to be ordained. They may never," Father Penance said, adding that last comment almost under his breath.

"Oh?"

"Yes, they are 'happy' being deacons. The orphans will be here for a short time, we hope," Penance said, changing the subject. "Every two months or so we have some wagons come in and we send them to Portland or Spokane. Perhaps you will be fit enough to join them and continue on your path."

"Spokane sounds about right," Swoop lied, but not

wishing to return ever to anywhere northwest, Portland or otherwise. "How can I repay you for…for all this?"

"Just say your prayers my son. Speak well of us out there, wherever you go. Perhaps write a nice letter? We need support for our mission."

"I'm not much for praying, Padre, it hasn't worked out well for me at all. But I will sing your praises. In the meantime, I'll get a bit stronger, and I will do some work here, any work you need done. But my feet. It's hard to stand, but I can do something. Do you by chance have anything to read?"

"I have a bible, but it is in Spanish."

"That'll do me no good."

"And there's a book. "Around the World in Eighty Days."

"Can't read Spanish, but I'd sure like something to read so the world travel book would keep my mind busy," Swoop said. "The Indians took my two books."

"Oh, one a bible, I hope?

"No sir. Fraid not. Two books on Stoicism."

"Oh, I see. I will get the world travel book to your room. It is not like a travel book. It is a fun adventure story by a man named Jules Verne," Penance said. He nodded and stood with his empty coffee cup.

"Need more?" he asked.

"No thanks." Swoop said.

He walked off to the metal urn over a small fire.

Swoop looked up at the orphans. Some looked back.

He saw a black-headed, teenage girl staring at him. The only one who dared to so far. She cut her eyes over to the preoccupied Penance then back at him, and clearly, silently mouthed two words…

"Help us."

Swoop squinted. A chill came over him. She looked away when Penance returned to the table. The priest spooned up a pile of sugar. He picked some very tiny bugs out of the spoon and tossed the sugar into the coffee.

Church bells sounded.

"Oh, oh I must go. New people or…or trouble at the church," Penance said.

"Trouble? I'll go with you," Swoop said, trying to get up fast, but several pains stopped him. With a groan, he used his arms on the table to brace himself up. Swoop limped after Father Penance, trying to catch up as they left the mess hall and crossed the big courtyard and entered the church. The Father won that race and beat him in by a minute.

At the church doors, Swoop saw the guard Svenson talking with a gaunt pair, a dirt-covered man and woman. Penance, then Swoop approached them.

"Twins," Svenson told Penance.

"Yes," the man said. "A boy and girl. Very sad. Teenagers."

Swoop stepped to the doorway and looked out to see a small wagon train of some 15 wagons stopped in a line out on the river road. They were a tired looking, ragged lot.

"Three days ago, it happened," the skinny man who was dressed like a poor farmer said. "Twins were happy, walking along behind their parent's wagon. Then…we were all on a narrow trail…the wagon…well, she just tipped over. Not a bad slope much at all, you know, not like a cliff or anything, but oh my sweet Jehovah, it started to roll over and over, on down the hill, screaming horses and all. It rolled about 4 times! When we got down there by them when the rollin stopped, the Grishams, they was all dead inside. Him, his mother and wife. Just…just all crushed up they were.

Wagon bashed half to bits. They went fast, thank Jehovah, they did. Noooo suffering, we think by the looks of them. We buried them out there. The two horses? The two horses lived! Ain't that something? They just rolled over a bunch still attached to the tongue. We let them loose and they got right up and started munching grass like nothing happened a-tall.

Swoop saw the teenage twins, both towheaded, as they stood outside looking in. They waited beside two wooden chests on the ground. Next to them were the two black horses, their reins tied off on a rail. One horse had a saddle, one didn't.

Deacon Ambrose appeared next in the church and walked up to them, also responding to the first bells.

"Well, Janet and Luke Gresham out there, well, they ain't got nobody no more," the traveler continued. "We're all from Indiana and they ain't got nobody left but a sorry cousin back home, but he pulls the cork and he ain't worth a stinking got-damn! I mean…sorry Father," he said after the curse word. "They ain't got nobody, no more."

"Not a problem. That is a very sad story," Penance said.

"No kin for the chill-ren'," the man continued. "We passed a farmhouse back aways, the Lotskys, and they said your church will help orphans. No one here on the train, well, we ain't able to accommodate them. We is barely getting by our own selves. And we got quite a long ways to go yet. We figured we'd gather up their trunks of clothes and things and get them here with the horses. We all could use the horses, yeah, sure. But we all thought it best that the chill-ren' keep them horses. Theys family horses. The kids might be worth more, you know to their adoption, if the horses came along with them."

Father Penance nodded through the whole story. Svenson remained speechless. Ambrose crossed his arms and eyed the twins up and down, and when he did cross those arms, Swoop could see the bulging outline on the hip of a holstered pistol under his black jacket when he did.

"We'll take care of them. Get them a home," Penance said. "Svenson help them with those chests."

Svenson grimaced at the suggested order. He looked back at Ambrose and Ambrose nodded at him to help.

Swoop walked out to the horses.

"Hi. Hi there, critters," he told them and stroked and hugged each of their necks, even smelled of them. Such was the connection of a veteran cavalry man and their animals. He looked them over for injuries, trying to imagine them toppling over and over down a hill. They were tough, big working horses and looked fine, even with a few minor cuts.

The twins watched him examine the horses like a veterinarian.

"They have names?" Swoop asked them.

"Classy and Sassy," Janet Gresham said.

Swoop nodded, repeating their names, "Classy and Sassy."

Then he looked over the battered wagon train on the river road. They were not unlike the various wagon trains he was once ordered to protect while in the Army from time to time. Or they looked like the wagon trains he was told to search for, that had "disappeared" on the trail, only to find the entire trains ravaged, tortured, dead men and raped women and children scattered about and within. The Comanches were the worst at it in his memory. He was even ordered to protect wagon trains on some occasions, if government officials were in transit, or influential friends of government officials were on the train.

Fifteen wagons were a small lot, as Swoop had seen as many as 100 such wagons in trains. Many of the wagons were delivering commercial goods along with families seeking the new digs and dreams of the west. Someday he knew that coal and steam engine trains would do all this slogging work. Right now, the wagons were pulled by horses and oxen. Swoop had read in the Chicago newspapers that oxen hauled half or more of the wagons across the United States and he believed it.

He thought about leaving the church right then and there, asking someone on the wagon train to take him somewhere, anywhere but Portland, but realized that if they couldn't even caretake these healthy twins, they wouldn't want his sickly self either. No, he was stuck at this church-fort-orphanage for a while longer.

The couple left the church and Penance ushered the twins inside by their shoulders. Swoop watched the couple board their wagon.

"Wagons Hoooo!" The wagon master up front gave the order to move on. He waved at him in a half-salute. Learning to hide every aspect of his military life and habits, Swoop just shook a pointy finger in the air.

With much rattling and shakes, they all slowly passed by, all glaring at the church and Swoop with the same interest as he looked back at them. Each wagon had a life story and an unclear future. He leaned against the front wall. Some waved at the twins still standing just inside the doors and the twins waved back. The two kids were in a state of quiet shock.

Once back inside, Swoop saw that Ambrose and Svenson had opened the twin's two chests and were handling items inside like they were at a rummage sale. Swoop stepped closer. One chest had a lot of jewelry in particular, several silver ring bracelets atop clothes and books. The other chest had quite a metal-studded gun belt and revolver. Ambrose picked it up, admired it and removed the long-barreled pistol for a better look.

"Your daddy a gunfighter or something?" Ambrose asked.

"No sir," Luke Gresham answered. "That belonged to his older brother. My uncle was a lawman in Evanston, Illinois. He was killed in the service. They mailed us his particulars. And the gun belt came with it."

Ambrose nodded and dropped the gun rig back into the chest.

"Get Sister Lamay," Ambrose told Svenson. Then he

turned to the twins. "Sister Lamay will get you set up. We'll ahhh, we'll…lock these chests away for you. We have a stable out back and we'll take care of the horses. Yup."

Swoop suddenly felt a little dizzy and stumbled an inch or two to the side and against the doorway. Penance looked at him, eyes wide.

"Okay?"

"Best lay down for a while, I reckon," Swoop said.

"Best," Penance said.

Chapter 9: Pat Weeps, the Ditch Digger
Omaha, Nebraska...

"Ditch Digger Bail Bonds, Pat Weeps speaking."

"Pat?" the voice asked on the telephone.

"Yup."

"Pat, it took me about 6 telephone dispatchers to get through to you. How are you. This is Gilliam Gray."

"Yeees, Gill, howdy doody. You still with Wells Fargo in St. Louis?"

"Oh yes! Still! Listen, before we get cut off here, you Ditch Diggers bounty hunters still got an itch yall can't scratch about that renegade general feller Swoop Swellen?"

"Hell, yeah we do," Weeps said.

"Listen up. A company of our guys up in Portland had some gold dust come a missing while in route from Alaska to Portland. Not the first time, so they hired us to investigate…"

"Yeah…"

"And we sent 10 agents out there. Sniffing around. They carried some new wanted posters with them. Per usual. One of the gold rush transportation guards up yonder? Looked like he was probably that wanted dead or alive general you want. He was going by the last name of June. The poster looked just like him. He was mysterious and all to everyone. He never spoke about his past history to anyone, but everyone he worked with said he had 'army' written all over him. Born and bred leader. A real fighter too wence needed."

"Did he fight like an angry madman?"

"That's the gossip."

"That's Swellen." Pat Weeps said.

"Yes! Well, our men were investigating some lost gold dust on a ship delivery, when this guy we think was Swellen left lickety-split. Just before they were going to interview him. Gone. He didn't steal any of the dust, cuz they quickly found out it was some of the sailors what did the stealin."

"Swellen may be a lot of things, but he ain't no thief," Weeps said.

"But they wondered why this June guy left. The only-est thing they could think of was they thought Swellen left was he was scared a being identified. He packed up and fled east on horseback. Middle of the night. Going east."

"He did? Uh-huh."

"Five of our agents, thinking at first, at the time he might be the thief, and well, shit…shit…dreaming too of the $1,000 reward too, chased after him. You know our boys can keep reward money if'n they catch somebody like that in the course of their duty, and Wells Fargo gets a cut of it too. So, they took off east after him, and Pat…that was almost three weeks ago and we ain't heard a hide ner' hair of the five since."

"Almost three weeks! You think Swellen killed all of

them?" Pat Weeps said.

"We think probably. Yeah. Maybe? Hinjins' maybe? It is unlike them to go this long without checking in. It's a real mystery, Pat. They must be dead. Just ain't natural for them."

"That figures, Gill. That…that figures. Swellen is one wily bastard. And he is capable of anything. Even killing five men. Especially if he gets mad."

"I figured I'd tell you fellers the news. All we know is that he and our agents headed off chasing him into eastern Oregon areas. We don't have the proper manpower to do much more right now. I'm gonna contact and send Colonel "Calico" Reams out there…you heard of him?"

"Oh yeah. Calico's a good man. I remember words about him in the Army."

"You know Calico is also a Federal Marshal. Got him a badge from some connection in Washington D.C. He's on their Marshal payroll, scant as the money is, and we have him on our Wells Fargo payroll too. It's very handy having a marshal among us at all times."

"I'll bet."

"We got Calico and two of his team right now working out in a Portland and Seattle investigation. Investigating pirates robbing and even stealing gold, supplies and now boats. Yukon Outfitters and other companies have jointly hired us. We are going to break that off for a while and send Calico and his team out East as soon as we can contact him and tell him to go and sniff around for our missing men. I figured I'd call you and tell you about Swellen and maybe you all might go after him up-ere' too, maybe find out something about our missing agents too. We don't have enough men for the job."

"Okay, Gill. We will. Can you telegram us the names and descriptions of the 5 missing men? Swellen might pretend to be one of them at some point. Might use one of their badges for ruse or something like that."

"Be looking for the telegram, we'll get it going. Tell yer boss man Jerry Pickwirth a big hello for me."

"I will," Pat Weeps said and duly excited, put the receiver down on the hook, disconnecting the call.

"JERRY!" Pat Weeps called out to Ditch Digger Bail and Bounty company boss in his main office. "Swoop Swellen may be in Oregon or a bit east."

Chapter 10: Last, the High Canyon, Hobo Man

Days passed quietly. Swoop healed a bit. Strength some-what returned. In the sunlight of the small window, he read from the Jules Verne book "Around the World in 80 Days." The protagonist Phileas Fogg bets he can make the global journey, but since he resembles a wanted bank robber, Fogg is pursued by Scotland Yard. Swoop, being a fugitive himself, found the plot both intriguing and depressing.

At times he closed the book on his chest and thought of the teenage girl who mouthed the words, "Help us." He stared at the cobwebbed corner of the room wondering, "What was that about? Why?"

Then three nights later, the peace was broken. There came the noise, the threats and the yelling. The catcalls, shouts and war whoops from outside started about mid-night, from all around the locked compound walls and doors. Swoop's eyes popped open and listened for a mo-ment, getting his bearings. He'd heard this all before, dif-ferent from different tribes in different forts he'd been in. It was a classic Indian siege, a verbal, psychological, terror tactic. He got dressed and limped down the hall to the church.

Deacons Ambrose, Penance, Svenson, Munday and several others were already there in the church, and Svenson was about to remove the wooden barricade that held the two big front doors locked.

"Don't!" Swoop shouted at him, hobbling in.

They all turned to look at him.

"There's nothing you can do right now by going outside," Swoop said. "This is a siege tactic to terrorize. They will do this for a while to create terror. We have time to plan right now. I need some guns."

Swoop was surprised to see Father Penance already armed with a pistol belt! The priest took off his gun belt and handed it to Swoop.

"You seen this mess before somewhere?" Ambrose asked, seemingly stressed and ready to surrender his command.

"Oh yes. All over. Get all the nuns and deacons armed and standing by those boxes by the walls, ready to overlook the wall. Get some in the church, the stables and dormitory rooftops. Get men on the stable roof to watch the stable gate doors to the outside. They could burn these doors and get in. These here doors too. Tell them to look around and report to me what they see when I get around to them," Swoop said while inspecting the priest's pistol. "Give every teenager a machete and tell them the truth about what might happen. This is a raid! At some point we will probably be raided."

"Probably?" Penance said.

"Probably. Sometimes Indians do this just for terror. For…fun. Yeah fun. Surround a farmhouse, even a small town, a fort, then laugh it off and leave. Or… they might attack or steal right then, or come back later, attack and steal and kill, later. Sometimes they capture someone, which is why we cannot go outside. They capture and torture someone outside and make them scream and scream for the trapped, sieged insiders to hear. Catch them a soldier. Husband. Wife. Child. Now with us here, I think it's a damn preamble for an attack."

"In the past, they have surprise attacked and stole things, killed a few church people," Penance said. "And since I've been here, they have pulled some real shenanigans, sneaking in at night, and stealing. But…not this… not all this yelling."

"Yeah. Go! Get everybody together in the courtyard and warn them. Svenson stay right here and watch this door. They'll ram it but probably set it afire," Swoop warned.

"Ve get vater ready?" he asked.

"Good idea. Why not, but the fire will be quick, hot and fast and they'll be kicking the doors in the whole time. Best get settled in and ready to shoot than carry buckets. A door fire will only burn the doors since the walls are adobe."

Outside, the war whoops and yells were louder and frightening to all, especially the orphans. Some of the threats were in English. Within 20 minutes all the children and all the staff were gathered in the yard. It didn't matter that Ambrose was standing right there, Swoop immediately, naturally took charge.

"This is the beginning of a probable attack," Swoop shouted out to all, "but we don't know when. Could be any minute, could be in a day or two. We need two shifts of guards, nuns and deacons on the walls, one shift watching, one shift resting and sleeping below, to change every 8 hours. Ambrose, you organize that. The sleepers will bed down by the walls, ready to respond. Keep your heads low when peeking over the walls and roof edges. They will be waiting to shoot yer heads right off or stick an arrow in them. We'll need lots of coffee brewing all the time. Meals brought to the walls."

Nuns were bringing out machetes from the work shed and laying them in a pile.

"You kids," Swoop continued, "you kids…each teenager take up a machete. You may have to kill to save your life. Now, let's go! Go!"

Swoop ran to a wooden box by the front wall and climbed aboard. The pain in his feet had gone from the adrenaline of the moment. He peeked over the immense, now somewhat cloudy night landscape, the flowing river, distant mesas, small mountains, the flat lands and the half-moon above. He could see no enemy out there as they were all concealed behind the slopes, ridges, brush and steep parts of riverbanks.

He dropped down, ran across the yard and climbed atop the dormitory roof. He listened and studied the surroundings. He determined the west wall, the wall with the stable doors, offered the most, close cover, and an invasion from that side would be fast. He would warn the west wall and stable guards of this threat.

He listened to the threats in English…

"Everybody dies bleeding slow, slow!"

"Woman and children, you are ours!"

"Die slooooow or surrender."

"We will butcher you like buffalo. Like cows."

…were some of the words he heard, among the war whoops and wild, animal sounds and chants.

Swoop knew they would also do these terrorizing vocals in shifts. There were more braves out there than just the voices heard. A second shift of yellers would take over. From his study, he guessed that outside each of the four walls had three or four callers, about 12 to 16 at work, maybe a little more, or a little less. And there would be a… shift change.

Swoop climbed down from above and walked into the

stable in the far northwest corner, his first visit to this barn. It was huge with 12 horses, mules and goats. There were two arched wooden doors to the outside. One Deacon stood guard in there.

"What's your name, troop?" Swoop asked him, slipping off into army jargon.

"Anderson."

"Anderson, you smell smoke, see a torch? Yell out to us. They might burn their way in here. It's very likely."

"I will," the man said.

Then something odd in there, up against the back wall of the barn caught Swoop's eye. There in a far corner was a metal wagon, a big cage on wheels, like a prisoner wagon that lawmen would transport a lot of prisoners in.

"What's that prison wagon doing here?" he asked. "I don't know," Anderson said.

"Tell you what, can we push that wagon in front of these stable doors? That'll slow them down if they try to get in, burn their way in."

"We can, yeah," the guard said.

"Let me help you," Swoop said, and the men set about turning the tongue left and right for the best angle and pulled and pushed the big cage on wheels in place just inside and across the stable doors.

"What's this prisoner wagon here for anyway?" Swoop asked.

"I ahhh…I don't rightly know," the man said. "It's ahh… always been here since we got here."

Swoop had an odd feeling the man was lying, but now was not the time to worry about it.

Just about mid-morning, all the chattering stopped. And one voice became clear outside the church doors on the river road. Swoop, Ambrose and Penance pulled more boxes up to the front wall, climbed up and peeked over the top to see who it was.

A lone, tall Indian stood on the river road. Swoop recognized his missing, stolen gun belt and two Thunderer pistols on his hips. He felt his heart race red with anger at the sight.

"Son of a bitch," Swoop growled like a monster.

"I am Nerto of no tribe. A new tribe, my tribe," the man yelled. "We want food, all your women and girl children. Nuns too. We will make a whole new tribe with your women and children. And…and we want the sick, high canyon hobo that walked here days ago. We know he is here. We tracked him here."

Ambrose and Penance looked at Swoop. Swoop stared ahead.

"If you do not give us this, we will come in and take them, and kill the rest of you. Or you give us what we want, and we will leave. You have until the high noon sun to decide."

"Should we answer? Say something?" Father Penance whispered.

"No," Swoop said.

Nerto backed away to the riverbank and dropped down out of sight.

"Why you?" Ambrose said.

"They left me for dead out there, and I did not die. They must want me dead," Swoop guessed, also trying to figure out the real reason why. It had to be the bounty. Did the Wells Fargo agents have a wanted dead or alive poster of him in their stolen gear? Probably. If so, would they alert the church people about it? Probably not, wanting the reward money for themselves.

The three jumped back down. All the orphans heard the threats and Swoop could tell they were scared to death, eyes wide, all looking at them. He walked over to them.

"We will do everything to keep them out, kids," Swoop said. "But if bad things happen, you will have to pick up our guns and pick up the fight. But we are here to protect you."

"Oh no, you're not!" Janet Gresham called out in anger.

This response surprised everyone. All the orphans, nuns and deacons knew what she meant, but Swoop didn't, and he just stared at her, confused. Then he saw a bruise on her face, on her right cheek and all around her right eye.

"Now you all go back inside the dorm," Sister Rosalinda ordered, and with a rifle in her hands herded them into the dorm doors. Swoop noted that she put the stock on her hip, barrel skyward like an old rifle hand, while barking instructions. But Swoop was too distracted to think about the look and remarks for long, and turned back for the church. Ambrose and Penance followed him.

Svenson and a deacon stood in the church foyer by the locked doors. Swoop eyed the deacon up and down, and the man noticed the inspection.

"And you are?" Swoop asked of a deacon.

"George Munday…a deacon…ahhh, Deacon Munday," he volunteered without a request for his name. We met days ago."

"Yeah. Deacon Munday, your guns? I need them," Swoop told Munday, looking down at Munday's two-gun pistol belt.

"Huh?"

"I'm going out there and I need your two pistols. Here you can have my gun belt for a bit. Your guns work? Clean em?"

"Uh…yeah. They be cleaned."

"Good, Gotta have em. Let's go. Let's go with them," Swoop snapped his fingers several times.

Munday reluctantly took off his gun belt and handed it to Swoop, in trade for Swoop's single gun belt.

"This is actually Father Penance's gun," Swoop said,

"In case I don't make it."

"Make what?" Ambrose said.

"Make this," Swoop said as he put the belt on.

"You…going out there?" Ambrose asked.

"Yup," Swoop said.

He pulled the brace of pistols and looked them over. He walked to the center of church, raised the guns and fired both once, from the hips, hitting two of those bad wooden religious statues, splintering them to pieces, like a sharp-shooting expert.

"Good. Just checking," Swoop said, and he reloaded the missing rounds in the guns. Those nearby stood aghast, both from his announcement and the hip-shooting, destruction of the two left and right statues.

Then Swoop told Munday, "Tell everyone on the walls outside, if and when the shooting starts, tell them to kill off everyone they might spot."

"Ahhh. Shootin' gonna start?" Munday said.

"I think so. If so? Shoot em. Dead," Swoop added.

Munday left.

Swoop lifted the wooden slat from the doors and opened one of the two front doors.

"I'm coming out to talk, Nerto," Swoop shouted out to the landscape. "Make a deal. Parlay! Treat!"

"Come then," the concealed Nerto shouted.

"Cover me," he told the stupefied Svenson and the Swede took up a position by the open door.

Swoop stepped beside Svenson and his at-ready rifle and then marched out of the open church door. He took a deep breath, looked around and half-smiled.

"Okay! Let's treaty!" Swoop yelled. "Let's talk!"
Nerto and another man walked into view on the river road before him. Two other Indians appeared also and stood beside them on each side of the duo, making four in a close row, All the other Indians in their band that still surrounded

the compound remained hidden, but two others stood up and stayed a distance away at each far front corner of the compound, at their ready. Six of them were in view, now expecting some sort of pow-wow talk.

Swoop walked within 8 feet of the 4 abreast men.

"I see you are wearing my guns," Swoop said to Nerto.

"I am Nerto. They are my guns now."

"Maybe for just the next minute," Swoop said, his eyes searching around them. Nerto did not absorb the threat.

Now closer to the river, Swoop looked over the incline toward the riverbed. He counted 9 Indians kneeling there and one of them was Sagiswatch.

"I see you over there," Swoop said, then turned back to Nerto, "you have the second Indian that left me for dead in the desert," Swoop said, "Sagiswatch."

"Aha! Ha!" Nerto said. "We know who you are, renegade general Swellen. We saw the papers of the Wells Fargo agents. The wanted poster. Now, we want you, the $1,000 and we want all the women in the church. And the food. Or else everyone inside will die. If you give us this, your men here will at least live."

Swoop grunted and said, "The food is terrible. The nuns ugly. The kids worthless."

"Ha, you say. The poster we have on you said you are wanted dead or alive, so if we kill you now, we still get the $1,000, and then we will still take the women and food after you are dead anyway. You have no choice."

"No choice? And that's why I came right out here," Swoop said.

"Why?" Nerto said.

"Kill you first," Swoop said.

In a second, maybe less, Swoop pulled both his pistols, about belly high. First, he simultaneously gut-shot Nerto and the man next to him, then shot them again a little higher in their chests. Two rounds into two. As they fell back from the sheer close blasts and pelting rounds, Swoop spread his arms outward further and shot the other two nearby Indians beside them, about mid-height. One into each one. Swoop dropped to a knee before those two guards hit the ground. This all happened in about 3 seconds.

Shocked, the two Indians out by the compound corners lifted their rifles but fell under the barrage of cover fire from the compound walls and church doors.

Two Indians charged up from the river bank to face the trouble. They were too close to each other, and Swoop shot them, easily also. Two shots, both at once. One fell, one stumbled and Swoop shot the stumbler again in the head. Others from the riverside began to stand and appear to the deacons on the wall. As Swoop had hoped, as commanded, steady gunfire from the walls erupted.

Swoop holstered his right-hand pistol, grabbed Nerto by his long head hair and drug him toward the front doors. Svenson shot from the doorway. The men and nuns on the walls killed any enemy they could spot. Swoop scrambled back inside, pulling Nerto as he shot with the gun in his left hand.

When Swoop and the dead chief made it inside the church, Svenson shut the door and barricaded it.

"You crazy…" Ambrose whispered.

Swoop unhooked his gun belt and handed it back to Munday.

"Thanks. Reload!" Swoop reminded Munday, almost in a sing-song manner.

Munday, also shocked, took the gun belt. Swoop stripped the corpse of Nerto of his Thunderers and put his lost gun belt back on. He pulled the pistols and checked the loads. Six rounds in each, his guns were unfired, and his belt loops still contained 18 rounds of .41 caliber bullets. He smiled.

"What now?" Ambrose asked.

"Well…we kill all those sons of bitches. Or they leave. They might leave now, with the wind out of their sails. Or get madder than hell, come forward right now. Or come back later, and…no matter what, we kill them."

Swoop turned to Munday, "tell the guys on the walls to keep shooting anyone they see, even if they are running away. Shoot em' in the back if they have to. They might regroup later, and we can't have that. And also, they might not leave."

Munday grimaced and looked at Ambrose.

Ambrose nodded.

"You…you done all this before?" Svenson asked.

"In a way. Kinda," Swoop said. He looked at his pants belt wrapped around Nerto's waste and saw Nerto's medicine bag attached to it. It was a big one. He removed it and opened the drawstring. He looked inside. Within were 5 Wells Fargo badges and a variety of smaller items like a tooth, a rock, a string of beads.

"What's that?" Munday asked.

"His powers," Swoop said. "Here Padre," Swoop said, pulling the thinner belt off of Nerto. He reached up to hand the bag to Father Penance. "It's got some badges of dead Wells Fargo detectives and someday you might give them to agents if they ever should pass by looking for their men."

Swoop knew they would.

"Vhat is that?" Svenson asked about the medicine bag.

"Some tribes call it a parfleche. We call it a medicine bag in English. It's a…something that gives them memory, power. Luck," Swoop said while he searched Nerto's pockets and found a folded piece of paper, which Swoop figured was his wanted poster.

He did not open it and shoved it in his jacket pocket. His verbal "pow-wow" with Nerto outside was far from the front door and no one in the compound could have heard the "$1000, wanted-renegade-general" statement

Nerto threat. Nerto wanted the reward money, not alert the compound inhabitants of the prize.

"That was quite a job you did," Father Penance said.

"The timing was right," Swoop said. "They had just given us their demands and they had it in their minds we'd all be thinking about the demands for a while. That we'd talk with them. Just good timing. A surprise."

"Well, I think more than that."

"Yeah. Maybe. That and luck, Padre. But they are still out there. With a mission to get in. This is not over. Not yet. Now…where can I get some socks around here?" Swoop asked.

"Mister High Canyon Hobo, by God, you can have my socks," Father Penance said.

Chapter 11: Lord's High Canyon Parish, the Attack

After the shooting and all the whooping and catcalling died down, Swoop retreated to his room. He opened the folded paper from Nerto's pocket. There he was, still wanted on paper, dead or alive for $1,000, his face drawn from that old Fort Shannon photograph. The same wanted poster he'd last seen in Colorado. Unfortunately, the artist did a great job replicating him. It was almost like a tintype photograph. He tore the paper into tiny strips and shoved the pieces back in his pocket. He would soon pass a fire and burn even the tiny pieces. Exhausted, he fell asleep.

And at 2 a.m., there was a fire and not the kind he wanted, but an ambush, surprise blazing. Apparently, the guard on the barn-stable roof fell asleep or some Indians were very stealthy. The dried-out, old wooden stable doors to the outside were set afire.

"FIRE!" Deacon Anderson guarding the inside of the stable cried out.

Those awake on the wall, atop their boxes turned to the stable. As soon as they all did turn, arrows zipped through the air at them. One arrow struck a deacon in the back of the head. He fell from his box face first, as Swoop rushed out into the courtyard and saw the man fall. He dashed to the dead man and picked up his lever action rifle.

"Watch your posts! Look outside! All sides! This is part of a trick. Reserves, follow me!" Swoop yelled.

The reserve shift of deacons and nuns, resting on the ground beside the boxes, scrambled with Swoop to the stable. Once there they saw the outside stable doors aflame but also that the prisoner cage wagon was still in position inside the opening.

"They'll be surprised to see that!" A deacon said, also surprised himself at the strategy.

"Yup," Swoop said. He knelt and raised his rifle to aim at the doors. The others saw this and did also.

The attackers kicked at the remains of the two blazing doors, shooting sparks and cinders everywhere. Unburned parts of the doors hit the wagon. When the dry doors disappeared, they stepped forward to see this cage, and they were indeed surprised to find the metal wagon barrier impeding their entry.

"Fire!" Swoop ordered.

And they all did, killing anyone in view, in the big, now empty smoldering, door frame, at least 5 of them went down.

One crawled under the cage between the wheels and was shot dead there.

"Hit the walls, look alive!" Swoop then commanded, as he knew the fiery breach was indeed a breach, yes, but also a main diversion.

"You two stay here and kill anything that tries to get in," Swoop ordered.

The enemy assaulted from all sides. Arrows flew into the compound. Their gunfire erupted. Swoop ran to the dead deacon with the arrow in his head and searched his pockets for rifle ammo. He found a box of loose rounds in a pocket. He reloaded the rifle.

An Indian flew over the 10-foot tall, back wall as though he was a flying monster, right between two wall guards, the native obviously hoisted and tossed in the air by outside accomplices. Swoop shot him dead when he landed. Another appeared airborne and Swoop shot him right out of the air. He flailed like hit by lightning, and landed headfirst.

Then Swoop climbed on the dead man's empty box to peer over the south wall and assess the situation. There were some 10 men shooting guns and arrows at them from this view, but the steady return fire from the deacons and the nuns was thinning them out. Then his eye caught the rolling red color on the ground outside the church front doors to his left. Those church doors were also set afire like at the stable.

He ran to the church and saw the chaotic skirmish inside. Shootings and hand to hand combat. Swoop dropped the rifle, took out his two Thunderers and charged in. An attacker, knife in hand, was fighting with Ambrose. Swoop shot him in the head. An arrow blew by Swoop's ducking head, and he shot the archer. Two Indians charged Svenson, pinning him against a wall, his rifle trapped across his chest. Swoop half circled them, clearing possible bullet paths away from the Swede. He shot the two down, leaving Svenson unscathed. Ambrose and the Swede were too shocked to even thank him. Penance was partially concealed in the pews with his revolver in hand trying to shoot anyone charging through the burned-out door frame. The freed men regrouped, and they took back the church. With Swoop free and afoot, he was able to move and shoot the enemies until the assault in the church came to a grisly end.

Then a gasping Ambrose and Svenson nodded a bewildered thanks to Swoop, as Swoop reloaded his pistols, then picked up his discarded rifle. Deacon Munday charged into the church as the outside gunfire and war whoops started slowing down.

"They are about done, out there. Running," Munday said.

"Get me a saddled horse," Swoop told Munday. "Fast. Bring it here. FAST!"

Munday didn't question that command. Swoop loaded the rifle and said to no one in particular among these church survivors, "Rifles in combat need slings. These should have slings."

Munday quickly appeared with a saddled black horse, one of the Gresham horses, at the compound church, door. Swoop took the reins and walked the steed into the church, stepping over and around the dead and mounted it in an acrobatic leap. He handed Penance the rifle.

"You stay here," he told Svenson. "You all, get to the walls and cover me."

"You going….out, again…" Ambrose said.

"Yup," and Swoop ducked under the door frame and the horse and rider were outside in the cold, night air. He took off for the river.

The men ran to walls and shared standing boxes with each other as they watched this strange man, this Mister Charles Last, the "High Canyon Hobo," ride out on the road and to the river.

Visible out there to them at their height, in this dark landscape, fled the last of the attackers who had failed in their assault. They watched as this Mister Last charged them from behind and with a revolver in each hand, shot and shot them all down. With both hands busy holding guns, it seemed he controlled the direction of his horse by way of his twisting torso and legs alone. Stopping, starting, turning and killing.

They could not see from this distance the sheer rage on Swoop's face and the tears of raw anger streaming from his wide eyes, nor could they hear his growling, cursing and swearing.

Some attackers did escape, but there was moaning and howling, this time from pain not terror. Swoop circled the survivors, and then the downed and wounded were finished off. Swoop had to reload. The onlookers did not know Swoop was also hunting for Sagiswatch among them, and he could not find Sagiswatch as he dispatched each wounded attacker. The cries of agony stopped.

"Sweet…Jesus," Father Penance whispered while watching Swoop maneuver and eliminate, as his once calm river and mesa scenery turned into a killing ground. Blood ran down the river.

Chapter 12: Napoleon, the Warlord

Pistols reloaded, Swoop holstered his weapons and slow-walked the horse back up near the smoldering church front doors. Several deacons and nuns walked out to greet him and look around.

"We need to circle the compound and search for any more trouble," Swoop said. "Organize yourselves right now, load your guns and sweep the area. Collect any guns and ammo you can find."

Ambrose grasped the logic and took charge of that search mission. Father Penance approached Swoop, rubbing the horse's neck.

"How many did we lose?" Swoop asked.

"No orphans were hurt. But we lost three men and Sister Dasa. Without you, and…your, your timing…it would have been worse."

Swoop grunted with a half nod.

"You…you have done this before? This…this sort of attacked fort…" the priest asked.

"…problem?" Swoop finished the sentence for him. Penance nodded.

"I have," Swoop said and dismounted. "I thought I was through with all that, though. Just 2 or 3 of these Nerto men got away. But if we'd let the last of them go? Too many of them get away? They might come back again. We can't allow that to happen. This pursuit had to be done. Had to be me, again, I reckon. It's like a curse of mine."

"I understand," Penance said. "I too am in the cursed business."

"Yeah, look, this ain't over. Post those guards back again on the walls. A few less, sure. But you never know for a while. Napoleon once said, 'The greatest danger occurs the moment right after victory.' You know, when you relax. You let your guard down. You think it's over. Smart generals have counter-attack plans for just that celebration moment. There are a lot of smart Indians too."

"Napoleon," Penance repeated.

"Napoleon," Swoop said. "Maybe Clausewitz. I can't remember exactly."

"Clause...who are you really, Mister Charles Last?"

"You don't want to know," Swoop said, and Penance watched Swoop and the horse walk away.

Swoop led the horse through the church doorway. He pulled the torn pieces of wanted poster paper from his pants pocket and shoved them between two burning boards laying on the ground from a front door. The shredded wanted poster curled up into smoke ash. He and Classy, or was it Sassy, left the church and out into the courtyard, where some wounded deacons and nuns moaned and squirmed under the help from their comrades.

Sister Rosalinda ran to him on his way back to the stable and asked, "What will we do with these dead Indians in here?"

"Outside and inside, we'll burn them. A warrior's end. Some Ute's wrap them up and bury or drop them into crevices in the rock or land. I understand they'll put a dead chief on a horse, kill the horse and bury both of them. But I believe up here they burn the body. This part of the country I'm pretty sure they build a mortuary cabin and set it afire, or…or they put them in canoes on a lake and burn the boats. I don't see how we can get all those canoes. And that's for lakes anyway.   The river outside won't do. We'll make some sort of a cabin maybe, start a big bonfire outside and burn them. Pull them all in a pile outside."

Swoop looked the grounds over.

"The orphans don't need to see all this," he said.

"They already have," she said, nodding toward the dorm windows and doors.

And sure enough, the kids and teens were all struggling for the space to look out, their jaws dropped, faces shocked. Some were crying.

"Maybe it's over, kids!" Swoop yelled.

"So, we burn these bodies?" she said.

"Yup. Cremate. They say their smoke raises them up to their afterlife. All these Indians here? These were renegades. Outliers. Criminals. But very much warriors, none the less. Befitting for them all, every one of them."

He walked to the stables and watered the horse. Sassy, or was it Classy, performed so well. The horses, goats, sheep and mules had calmed down from all the earlier fire and bullets. Anderson the guard, watched him with little glances his way, of shock and awe.

Swoop knew he could not stay at this church-orphanage for very long. This news would eventually get out, not too quickly, but it would spread, about the maniac Mister Last, how and what he did and the way he did it. Words would spread, then hunters would hunt, and he needed a head start beforehand.

Feeling exhausted, feeling the ache in his feet return again, even with Penance's socks on, he walked to each wall, stood on a box and examined the grounds and watched the men searching. The sun was just about to rise, and the eastern sky and clouds looked like a red clay line and a strip of fire on the horizon. All seemed under control.

He decided to help drag the Indian bodies outside of the courtyard. He grabbed the arms of the first inside man he shot who was thrown-leapt over the back wall. He wasn't very heavy, but the job was tiresome and tough at this hour. In a moment, all the nuns and deacons stopped what they were doing and watched him, as many of the orphans continued to cram into the windows and doors to see. At one point Swoop stumbled from his unsure footing and exhaustion.

Then some of the nuns and deacons walked over to the few dead inside the courtyard. They began pulling the bodies toward the church, through the church and out the front doors.

Outside they saw where, well east of the compound, Swoop laid the first body. They followed his path and did the same.

"The burning smell will be bad, best get them far enough away," Swoop warned. "If we don't burn them soon, the rotting smell will be worse."

Ambrose, Penance and Svenson watched and realized he was right. The compound outside was surrounded by death and the bodies have to be removed, and the smell would be wretched soon. The bodies had to be hauled off and collected in a distant location.

"Let's go," Ambrose reluctantly said. "We'll bury our guys and gal, but we have to do this too."

Within the hour the bodies started to pile up. Some on the ground and some in piles atop each other. Swoop counted 24. And none of them were Sagiswatch. He walked to the compound wall and sat, his back against the adobe wall.

Father Penance backed away from the mound and sat down on the ground next to him.

"I thought…Padre…" Swoop started in a tired, soft tone, "I thought I would never do or see such a thing as this again."

Swoop stared ahead at the nightmare pyramid of the dead.

"I thought I'd left all this in my past."

"You *were* in the Army, Mister Last," Penance said.

"That I was."

"Do you have anything you wish to confess?"

"Plenty. But not here. Not now."

"You will feel better, my son."

"Nothing…nothing will make me feel better. Ever. Some things are beyond better, beyond that."

They watched as the last body was dropped.

"Twenty-five," Swoop said, "Probably more in the river."

"It is ungodly to try and burn them."

"That's what they do in these parts," Swoop said, "their way. Their God."

"Our ways are better."

And Swoop just smirked and grunted at that.

"I'm gonna jump in that river and take a bath. Up from the dead. I stink of death and gun smoke. Then go to bed," Swoop said. "Make sure they collect all the guns and ammo, okay?"

"You have run out of bullets before, I presume?"

"Yes. In some forts and outposts, we were so desperate at times, between raids, we had to dig the slugs out of the dead. Melt them and reshape them. We had to "make our own bullets." I would always check on the post's supplies. We need lead bars, a melting ladle or small iron kettle to melt the lead in, a bullet mold suitable for particular guns, and either loose black powder and percussion caps, or brass cartridge jackets and primers. Good posts keep all this on hand for emergencies. 'Making your own' goes back to the flintlock days of war."

Page 93

Father Penance just stared at Swoop's profile.

Then Swoop unhooked his two-gun belt, walked to the river and stripped off his deacon clothes. Down to nothing he stepped in the Canadian mountain-based stream. It seemed just short of freezing, but he sat down in it up to his neck, rubbing his skin. He was upstream from his shooting and killing of those once fleeing. The rapid water surely washed them quite aways already. He ducked his head several times getting water over as much of himself as he could. Then he reached for and drenched his clothes, crushing and wringing them out with his bare hands.

When his body started to quiver, naked, he stood and hung the wet clothes on his shoulders. He ignored all the looks and leering especially from Rosey the nun who stared at him lasciviously. She picked up his gun belt and ran it over to him. He took it with a tired nod.

"I'll get these dry," she said.

He took to his room. He wiped the sand and dirt from his bare feet and sat on his crusty bed. He rotated his re-covered gun belt in his hands. He'd already shot up half his supply of .41 caliber bullets and either he found some more such ammo on the compound, or he'd have to switch guns. He'd clean his guns tomorrow. Surely, they had gun cleaning tools here at the church, what with all the gun-slinging deacons and nuns. He would run some hot, soapy water through the guns and dry them quickly. Maybe they had some grease or oil. Along with some kind of poker and textured cloth or brushes to help with cleaning.

Tomorrow! He laid back on his towel-pillow. There he thought about the bullets and arrows that just missed him by hairs. He thought about the dead. He thought about having to "swoop" in, again, one more time. And the aftermath. The bodies. All those bodies. The wanted poster. How foolish was he to leave his Fort Shannon post, go AWOL, Wounded Knee or no Wounded Knee. He finally fell asleep, for almost a full day.

At dinner time Sister Rosalinda burst into the room with his mostly dried clothes, acting more like a frisky "Rosey" than Rosalinda the pious nun.

Chapter 13: Chief Tante Ourau, the Chief's Chief

Knocking, then a voice…

"Might be more trouble outside. I don't know. Big trouble," Father Penance said while cracking open the door, with his head poked in the doorframe.

Swoop groaned and sat up, rubbed his face. He put on his still slightly damp, priestly clothes, then buckled his gun belt on.

He walked with a limp down the side hall and into the church and he saw several of the men standing outside the empty doorframe. He joined them.

"Look," Ambrose said.

There were more Indians, way, way more Indians walking toward them from across the river, but they moved slow and not quite in single file but close to one. Maybe as many as 50 of them! No weapons drawn, or up. Some were on horseback, some on foot. They saw the group had two big US Government wagons in the march with them.

The mounted men in the front waved at them.

"Peaceful?" Ambrose asked.

"I don't know," Swoop said. "But…those are government wagons they've got there. Letters 'U.S.' on the side. Clean white canvass. Maybe some hidden trouble? Put some men on the walls. Tell them not to show any guns yet."

With these fresh orders, Svenson took off. The line casually crossed the river with the usual struggle, getting within 20 feet of Swoop and his comrades. The group in the lead all wore big feathery, head gear, and what looked like clean, ceremonial clothes. They had tooled crafted saddles on their horses. Swoop knew these would be the leaders. Most all the others with horses to the rear were bareback.

A well-dressed front man in deerskin and leathers slid off his horse and walked up to them.

"Greetings," he started, "May I present to you Chief Tante Ourau of the Ute tribe," and with a sweeping hand of a nobleman, turned toward the elder chief on horseback.

Two other men dismounted and joined the greeter. The chief rode up, nodded and got off the horse under the watchful eye of these two other Indians afoot, as though ready to catch him if he fell. The chief did not stumble. He landed and walked up near the greeter, smiling at Swoop and his compatriots.

"Greetings, I speak English," he said.
Swoop immediately, naturally took charge. Ambrose didn't care. He was ill-equipped for all this.

"Greetings Chief Tante Ourau. My name is Charles Last," Swoop said, "would you like something to drink or eat?”

“No thank you, sir. I journey with so much food and water, I should offer you some of mine instead. The U.S. government has appointed me the chief of all northern Utes in the region.”

“I am a spokesman for this church and orphanage, Chief Tante Ourau,” Swoop said. “Would you like a chair, Chief?”

“Soon maybe Mister Last, if I decide to stay, but I will not bother you long. We were told by a scout of ours that one of our brothers, Nerto and his men were roaming in this area and that he has attacked your church and orphanage.”

“Yes, sir.”

“Unsuccessfully. I see that he has failed,” the chief said pointing to the body pile of carnage on the east side of the compound.

“Yes Chief. We are planning on creating a cabin of wood for them all and setting it afire, as I believe that is your final custom.”

“It is. Yes. One custom. How you know this?”

“I read a lot of books,” Swoop said.

The chief nodded several times.

“Nerto…Nerto wanted to become like the famous Geronimo. Causing trouble and stealing and killing. This is not our way,” he said.

“And it is not our way to kill any Indians, unless they cause trouble, stealing and killing. That is not our way.”

“Then these are both not our ways. This is good that we know this about each other. And give these words to each other. We have journeyed to find Nerto and ask him to return with us. Then our scout told us of this church attack.”

“Was your scout named Sagiswatch?” Swoop asked.

“No. No, but I know of Sagiswatch. He likes to travel around, and he knows many tribes and pioneers and settlers. He has a big nose to smell everything and a big mouth to tell everything. He makes many plans that I…we…don't approve of. You know? You have met him?"

"I have. Sagiswatch left me for dead in the canyon. Nerto and his men killed five of my friends and left me for dead in the canyons. Then Sagiswatch and Nerto came here to kill more people at the church"

"I see. You are a priest of your God?" the chief asked, pointing at Swoop's clothes.

"No Chief. When I was almost killed by Nerto days before this attack, I was stripped and left for dead in the desert canyons to the south of here. I made it here anyway. Somehow. I almost died. These people here gave me their extra clothes. Clothes of a religious man."

"I see. But then, clothes or not, you have been on a spiritual journey. A vision quest in the canyons."

"I…perhaps. Yes" Swoop said.

"It is important that you almost die. Did you see any visions?"

"I think so," Swoop said, "A few. I saw the ghost of my dead wife." Swoop was surprised he confessed this, blurted this out, but he seemed very connected with the Chief at the moment.

"Oh?" The Chief said, very interested as his head leaned in with a concerned face.

"She was an Indian, sir, from Minnesota. She appeared to me as a ghost laughing at me," Swoop said.

"Oh? Huh? This could mean many things. Laughing at you? Huh! Or laughing at the world? I am sorry I cannot help you without much more talking between us."

"I know."

"Perhaps this will become clear to you through time."

"Perhaps. The nightmare may have saved my life at the time though."

"Oh? Good then. I see. She warned you. We have our Godly ways. And we also have our death, ritual ways. We cannot have you do the work of such rituals of our brothers over there. Especially after they have attacked you. We would like to gather up these bodies, return them to our reservation, for our, as you say, funerals."

"I understand."

"Nerto was a problem, Mister Last, like a criminal, but some of these other men of his are beloved by their families. We live by a lake, and we will have a funeral there. Each in a canoe set on fire."

"I thought maybe that would be your way," Swoop said. "And we have so little wood here for a cabin and no canoes and no lake. I think that such a thing on a lake would be beautiful to see. I wish I could watch that. They fought very hard and bravely."

"As I can see. If you can, you may join us in peace and watch this."

"And no one will try to kill me in revenge?"

"Ahhhgh. I don't think so," the chief said with almost a smile. "All these men were trouble to us. But they are us. You know much, Mister Last. You were once married to an Indian woman. Have you also been in the military? The Army? You have a music to your voice with me, your words picked so we can speak together…they are carefully chosen words…like you have spoken with many Indians before and are wise about such things."

"No," and Swoop hated to lie to this chief, but he had to. He also did not tell him he was one-eighth Indian. He only repeated, "I read a lot of books."

"My men will collect the rest of bodies if you will allow us."

"Yes of course. Some have been shot in the river. And The water carried them away. East. Some were shot across the river,"

"I see. I will send some of my people in the river and down the riversides to search. Perhaps at a turn or a fallen tree we might find someone. Oh, the troubles they have caused, but they are us."

"Yes."

"It was very good to speak to you Mister Charles Last. Good music."

"Good music. And it was very good to speak with you, Chief Tante Ourau."

They stepped up to each other and shook very tight hands. The chief nodded goodbyes to the other men, turned, motioned with his hands in almost a unique sign language for the tribe behind him to move in and collect the dead bodies. The two Army wagons rode up to the pile of the dead. The chief walked back to his horse and with a little help from those two aides, he mounted the stallion. He turned the horse and with an entourage of feathered chieftains, crossed back across the river, passing the two big, U.S. government covered wagons.

Within minutes, The Utes began loading the bodies into the wagons. Eight of them on horseback walked in and by the river, looking for bodies. Others walked the riverside.

Chapter 14: Adrian Glance, the Indian Agent

Swoop seriously considered leaving with this tribe, to watch the burning canoe funerals, but what he spotted next ruined the idea.

A white man, dressed in a three-piece suit and short brimmed hat on horseback, trotted up between the body removers and the church, and when Swoop saw him, he knew he was in deep trouble. It was his old friend and Indian Agent, one Adrian Glance from his AWOL post command, Fort Shannon. This man most surely knew him and knew he was wanted.

Indian Agent Adrian Glance about fell off his horse seeing his old friend and compatriot, Lt. General Mordecai "Swoop" Swellen standing in front of an obscure church, dressed in preacher's clothes, in the middle of nowhere. He stopped his horse and dismounted. He approached the group and introduced himself.

"I am Indian Agent Adrian Glance, assigned to this part of the state. Came out here with the Chief, hoping to help out here in any way. We have been hunting for Nerto and his men, trying to quell them and bring them back home to the tribal lands. We heard about this attack, and we were too late. A scout or, you might say a spy of sorts, traveled back and forth from Nerto to us, told us what happened yesterday. We were nearby. And we see we are indeed too late."

He started shaking hands with each man and stopped in front of Swellen.

"And you sir? Your name?" he asked.

"Last, Charles Last," Swoop lied.

"Mr. Last, and you are a…priest here too?"

"No sir, I was left for dead in the desert by Nerto. They rescued me. I needed clothes."

"And thank God we did. He saved us all from Nerto's attack," Father Penance added.

"Hmm, I don't doubt that," Agent Glance said nonchalantly.

"How is it you are way out here?" Swoop asked, trying to change the subject.

Adrian Glance stepped back to tell everyone, "I was transferred here. Well, perhaps you all recall what the newspapers dubbed the Massacre at Wounded Knee in the winter of 1890? Gentlemen, I was the Indian Agency representative there for the Lakota. I myself, and a few others (he glanced at Swoop) knew beforehand, we could predict that what the Army wanted us to do would become a terrible mess, a bloody mess. Some of us didn't have the courage to leave beforehand…to…to not take part in all its inevitabilities," now he looked right at Swoop. "I was…and I was there, in it. I shot no one but saw it all happen.

After such a mess at Wounded Knee, though I was acting fully under government orders, they had to move me. I was transferred way further west. Out here. Dang lucky I wasn't fired."

Then nervous, Swoop wandered over to the Utes caretaking the bodies. After some conversation with the remaining church men, Agent Glance wandered over near Swoop. Alone, a few feet apart, they watched the slow removal of the corpses as they piled them into the Army wagons.

"Swoop," Glance said, looking forward.

"Adrian," Swoop said, looking the same direction. "You might need more wagons."

"You have created quite the vengeance trail for the Army," Glance said.

"Vengeance trail. That's one way of calling it."

"You look like hell warmed over," Glance said.

"I am warming up for hell. I was just about dead a few days ago."

"You're kind of a hero to some of the men at Shannon after the massacre. They understood why you left. When it was too late to support you. But you know the Army will kill you rather than let you have a public court martial."

"I thought that. You heard that?"

"I heard that gossip," Glance said.

"Yeah. Some. And I thought about that. A lot. How's Doris and the kids?" swoop asked.

"Fine. Things are a little sparse at Warm Springs, near the rez. But we've been sparse before. Winters are hell."

"Uh-huh. Winters were hell in the Dakotas."

"Don't worry, Swoop. I will not tell anyone where you are now."

"Thanks, Adrian, and I won't be here much longer anyway. I gotta move on."

"You kill that bounty hunter Gee Willikers in Colorado? I heard about."

"No, a woman killed him. He shot the woman. The woman shot him. I saw it. I didn't do it."

"Juuuust wondering. Some are wondering."

"Yeah. And if you hear that I killed any Wells Fargo agents? I didn't. Nerto and his men killed them. Five of them."

"Okay."

Something caught Swoop's eye in the body removals. He jogged over to the men.

"Hey, hey…" and Swoop motioned for Adrian to follow him, "this…this one there is wearing my clothes. My hat, my shirt, jacket and boots. Can I get them back?"
Adrian began talking with the two Indians that were pulling the dead man's body. They stopped and listened, and then waved their hands toward the corpse and stepped away to fetch another body. Swoop moved in and started undressing the dead man.

"There's some blood and two bullet holes in that flannel shirt and jacket," Glance said, leaning in.

"I don't care. I'll clean them. He didn't bleed too much, must a died fast. Then I'll sew those holes up. It's got to be better than these old padre clothes they gave me."

"Must," Adrian said and could barely conceal a laugh and smile. "I'd help ya, but it would look like we knew each other," he said.

"Heaven forbid," Swoop said, busy with pulling the boots off. "Some one of these sons of bitches got away with my life savings. $200. I wonder where that money is?"

"NOooo!" Adrian whispered, but with feeling.

"Yes. On that, I am not hopeful I'll find it here."

"That's a dang shame."

"Look. Look how polished these boots are. They look like new," Swoop said. "He took good care of them."

Glance stepped back, slowly reached into his pocket and one by one dropped silver dollars onto the ground, his hand close to his leg.

"I just dropped 6 dollars, Swoop. That's all I got with me. You take it."

"Thanks, Adrian," Swoop said, not looking up at him. "I will need it."

As they walked back to the church. Swoop kneeled by the silver dollars to fix his sandal and picked up the money.

Before they got too close to church, Swoop whispered out of the side of his mouth, "Tell Doris hi."

"I will," Glance murmured.

"My lost clothes," Swoop announced, holding them up, when they returned to the group.

It took about an hour to load the wagons. A grizzly job. They somehow did fit all the recovered bodies inside the two wagons. Adrian Glance mounted up and came by the front of the church.

"Goodbye gentlemen, have a fruitful life," Adrian Glance said, not looking at Swoop, and he rode off with the wagons across the river.

Swoop knew he could not leave with this tribe. He did wish to witness the Indian lake funeral rites and recuperate as invited. But, if anyone found out he did, and spent days close to Agent Adrian Glance, Glance would probably be crucified for some kind of treason.

"Last, I will tell you," Ambrose said to Swoop with a snort, "we were not going to build a cabin for them savages. We'd let em rot. And anyway, we don't have the wood for it."

That seemed to Swoop like a "the danger is over and put me back in place," a remark that Ambrose is still the boss around here, reminder.

"Good thing they came and got them, then," Swoop said staring ahead calmly, instead of punching Ambrose right off his feet. He felt his right hand form a fist, down at his side. The fist quivered. He controlled himself.

"And that rifle you picked up?" Ambrose continued with a rough voice, "From Randy. That's our rifle. And I want it back."

"Oh?" Swoop turned to him, with an impatient stare,

"it's back in my room. Why don't you just come and get it," in a tone that did not sound like an invitation at all. "Or, you'll get it back, one way *or* the other, when I leave."

Swoop walked off. The group nearby was silent, until Father Penance chuckled.

"I might suggest," the Father said, "you wisely select the 'or' part of that one. And leave him be."

Ambrose just leered back at him.

Chapter 15: Deacon Williams, the Threatener

"Sister Rosalinda," Swoop said, seeing her in the court-yard, "can you get the kids to wash these. I guess I will sew up the bullet holes if they don't sew."

"I will do it. And you know it's just Rose, baby. Because of our plans."

"Plans?"

"Yes, what you told me, when we..." she whispered.

"I told you some plans?" he interrupted, "I…I may have said something when I was feverish. Last week, I guess? I don't remember."

She smiled, "YOU! I will remind you later," she said and winked.

"Hey, that girl, the new girl. One of the twins. Janet Gresham. She has a big bruise on her face, and she cried out yesterday that…"

"Oh, she is a terrible girl. Fighting with the other girls." The nun said. "Ignore these kids. Just leave them be. They are all terrible. Each one of them little mayhems."

Then she turned away from him, his recovered, old dirty clothes in hand. He was confused that they'd made plans?   Confused about the orphans all being terrible? He watched her leave, then made for the orphan's dormitory building.

What did that one girl mean when she whispered, "Help us," from across the room. He decided to ask Janet Gresham herself about her bruises.

Inside the orphan dormitory, it stunk of feces and dirty feet. The uncirculated air hung thick in a dusty haze. The orphans were busy working on chores at rows of tables. Unkempt beds were far to the left of the big, open area. He spotted the twins alone, sitting on beds, facing each other. He approached them.

"Janet, can I talk with you?" he asked.

"No!" she said, not looking at him.

"What do you want?" Her brother Luke said with anger.

"I'd like to find out, to ask how she got that bruise on her face."

"What do you care?" Luke said. "Get out of here. Get away from her."

"Maybe we need to talk outside. Come on," Swoop said as he reached down to grab her wrist.

Luke jumped up and punched Swoop right in the face! Swoop took the blow, by twisting his head a bit with its force. Still, it was a pretty good shot for a kid. Swoop did not retaliate and somehow didn't even get mad, which was very odd for him. He just looked at Luke quizzically.

"What's…what's going on here?" he asked.

"You ain't taking my sister anywhere, mister. Nobody is."

Three nuns responded in a flurry of black and white.

"You should not be in here," one declared. "You must go. No contact with adults allowed!"

"I…"

"Go! Leave!"

And the three nuns grabbed Swoop's arms, pushed and shoved him out of the dorm, under the watchful eyes of all the other orphans.

They ejected Swoop out into the courtyard.

"Leave them kids alone," one deacon outside said. Swoop heard the deacon called Williams before and the man marched up close to him with a challenging expression. He was big and Swoop didn't like his aggressive march and immediately thought about an uppercut to jaw but took a deep breath instead. He just stared at the man.

"We have a rule here. No adults interact with the orphans, except the sisters," Deacon Williams said.

"Hmmm," Swoop growled.

"So, you stay away. You did a lot here, sure, but the rules? Them's the rules."

Swoop took a deep, deep breath, walked around him and returned to his small room. Dead Randy's recovered rifle was still propped up in the corner. Ambrose had not retrieved it. He sat on the sorry excuse for a bed and thought…

Where is Sagiswatch? The Indian surely knew he was wanted. What possible plans did he make with Sister Rose while he was feverishly near dead? What could you possibly promise a nun? And, did she just call him "baby?" And what happened to Janet Gresham? Something bad. Why did Luke Gresham haul off and punch him like that? Will agent Adrian Glance keep his promise and not tell the Army that he saw him in eastern Oregon? When will Wells Fargo send out more agents to find out what happened to their missing men? And finally, what? What's going on here with these orphans?

Chapter 16: Mr. Last, The Patron Saint of Donkeys and Mules

Sister Rosalinda barged into his room the next morning.

"Here's your clothes baby," she said in a sing-song.

Groggy, startled, naked, Swoop stood up. The nun dropped the pile of folded clothes on the bed and rushed him. She was a big, wide girl and quickly had him up against a wall.

"Hey, I…" Swoop started.

She kissed him and was forcing her tongue into his mouth. He untangled himself and slowly pushed her back.

"What…what kind of a nun are you anyway?"

"I'm a fun nun. You know that. When are we leaving here?"

"Okay. Okay. Tell me what we were talking about again? Planning. I am a little hazy, being near dead and all, about our plans. Us leaving."

He moved her to the bed and sat her down with two hands on her shoulders. He started donning the clean, sewed up and ironed clothes. She watched him move very closely.

"These men around here are not men like you."

"Like me? These men are all deacons. I reckon they will become priests. Haven't they all taken that vow?"

"That vow of celebracity?"

"Cela...ahhh, you mean celibacy," Swoop corrected, even more confused about her pronunciation and status. "Haven't you? Taken that vow? Aren't you married to God, or something?"

"I was married once, to an old man when I was 15 years old."

"Well, ain't that ripe," Swoop said.

"He died of consumption. Otherwise, I've never been married. God or nobody. I have told you my life story."

"You have? I don't remember. Well, Rose, Sister Rosy, I must have been drugged or half-dead. I don't remember your life story."

Swoop suddenly had a mental flashback of her sitting on top of him. Naked legs spread. Her nun robes pulled up high on her body. He shook the vision from his head. His eyes widened and his head jolted back an inch. Did that even…happen?

She just smiled.

"Are you a nun or…or not?" he asked.

"I am a bad nun if you want me to be," she said, tapping her thighs with her fingers. Those legs were spread apart under her habit, "and these deacons around here sure as hell ain't no celebrets."

"Cele…yeah. I will be happy to leave here," Swoop said, dressing, and buttoning his flannel shirt, "it's all too confusing."

"I'll be happy to go with you."

"Nooo, Rosy, you won't be happy at all. People are always trying to kill me."

"You said you are going to rescue me from this life," she said.

"I was delirious, almost dead. I think. I don't remember. I can't rescue my own self, least of all you too."

"You know that teen age boy that punched you, yesterday? He's done run away overnight. He's a runaway."

"A runway. The Gresham boy? When?"

"Middle of the night."

"How?

"I don't know. I guess, he ran out one of those doors what got burned down by the hinjins."

"His sister with him?"

"No."

"He take one of his horses?"

"No. No horses. All the horses and mules are still in the stable. Anderson sleeps in there and he was probably afraid he'd wake him."

"And his sister is still here?"

"Yup, I just said. Still here."

"Huh."

"Ambrose and some of the boys went after him. They'll likely to kill him."

"Kill him! Why?" Swoop declared.

"Kill him. Yeah. This place has some mighty big secrets, handsome. Like me. And if'n he knows any of them? Him getting away from us is a problem. Telling secrets."

"What secrets?"

"Secrets. I don't know," she said, shrugging her shoulders, "who's really who. What's really what? What's really goin' on round here. Those secrets."

Swoop pulled his boots on and buckled his gun belt. He grabbed the rifle.

"Where you goin, handsome?"

"Eating something. Hungry. Then for a ride."

"Ride? Can I go?"

"No."

He left for the mess hall. Breakfast was in session, and he laid Randy's rifle down on the staff table and snatched up a piece of white bread and spooned some scrambled eggs atop it. He did not sit to eat it. Then he downed a big glass of water. Father Penance watched him gobble all this down.

"Hurry?" Penance said. In such a hurry?"

"Yeah."

"For what?"

"Morning ride."

Swoop saw another nun walking around talking with the orphans and then he spotted…on that nun's wrists… those silver bracelets that were once inside Janet Gresham's trunk. Janet's mother's bracelets. She'd obviously stolen them and proudly wearing them.

"So nuns now wear fancy jewelry?" Swoop said as he pointed out to Penance the nun wearing the bracelets.

Penance just shrugged his shoulders.

Swoop saw Janet Gresham seated at a table on the orphan's side of the hall and he walked up to her and leaned in, putting his fists on the table.

"Your brother in some kind of trouble?"

"I don't know." Her eyes shifted left and right to see if anyone was looking at them.

"Where's he going?"

"I don't know." Her eyes still shifted left and right again.

Swoop grunted, left her and walked back over to Father Penance.

"What's going on with the new twin kids? The brother?"

"I don't know," Penance said.

"He ran away I'm told."

"I didn't know that," Penance said again.

Swoop retrieved Randy's rifle from the table and left the cafeteria.

A boy about 12 years old cautiously followed him outside. When they were both outside, the boy yelled to him.

"Hey, Mister Last! You gonna' hep' him?" The boy asked.

Swoop stopped and turned.

"Help who, son?"

"Luke."

"You think Luke needs help, young feller?" Swoop said.

"He needs hep'. We all need hep' here."

"I am starting to think now that I know you all do."

"But, not like you think. You know Oliver Twist?" the boy asked.

"Oliv…the story? The story by Dickens?"

"Yes, sir."

"That I do," Swoop said.

"It's worse here. You know Edgar Allen Pope?"

"You mean Poe. Edgar Allen Poe?"

"You know those Poe stories?" The boy asked

"Some," Swoop said.

"It's like that here. Not Twist. Poe stories. You read em'. You know. Only it's worse here. Way worse."

"What's your name son?"

"Foley Delane."

"Well Foley Delane, I might be doing something about that."

"You will?" Then he gave out his wishes, "Will you adopt me now? Please? Now? Rescue me from all this Poe? PLEEEASE?"

The kid's dirty face and crackling voice about broke Swoop's heart in just one second. He sighed and took a knee down next to him.

"I can't son. I…I am a mover. I have to move around and I can't have a home."

The boy lunged forward, hugging his neck and almost knocking him over.

"I'll move with you. I can move around too," he said.

"Sorry, kid. But if there is something I can do about kicking all the Edgar Allen Poe outta' this place? I'll try to do it. Now go on back inside before you get in trouble talking to me."

Foley Delane frowned and stepped back with a sad face. He wiped his eyes. He bowed his head, spun and ran back in. And just in time. The nun wearing the stolen silver bracelets was in the doorway, leering at him.

Swoop looked up at her.

"What's your name, Sister?" Swoop asked.

"Well…Sister Bloodworth."

"Sister Bloodworth? I didn't know that…that nuns liked jewelry," Swoop said and stood up, his eyes cutting down to the bracelets on her wrist and then back up to her impatient face.

"Jesus wore bracelets," she said.

"I didn't know that about Jesus either. Him wearing shiny, girly bracelets. But, I don't think he did."

She grimaced at him, spun and returned inside.

Swoop walked to the stables, but he heard some distant curses from a man inside before stepping in.

"You piece of shit, you…" a voice bellowed.

Inside, Deacon Anderson had his fists rolled up and was punching a donkey's side. Hard. Really hard. Once. Twice. Three times! The beast of burden shrieked out and honked with each blow.

"You…" the man complained.

"Hi," Swoop said loudly, popping up on the other side of the donkey. He rested his arms atop it, grinning. He still held Randy's rifle in his hands.

Anderson looked up at him.

"What you want?" he was in a questionable anger, trying to still sound tough but realizing that was dangerous in front of this madman, this Mister Last.

"I realized that you really don't know me," Swoop said.

"You're that High Desert Hobo them hunjins' wanted to kill. I know you. They came here to get you."

"Oh, yeah, some call me that. They call me Charles Last around here too, but that ain't my real name either."

The man stood up straight and glared at him.

"No sir, my real name is Patron Saint Jackass. I am," Swoop said, "Yup. And, I am the patron saint of all beasts of burden," Swoop said with a big smile. "Me and the Donkeys, the mules. Yup, you'd know that from the Bible. I reckon you've read the Bible?"

Swoop stepped around the hurt, beaten creature.

"I'll be around here a few more days and well…" (smile evolved to a sneer) if I catch you punching this donkey, a mule, or any animal in this stable I will take out this knife I've got here on my belt, and I will gut you into two fucking pieces."

"You can't…"

Swoop struck the man with the butt of Randy's rifle right smack in his face. The man fell back and down on the dirt. The donkey left the immediate area.

"Ahhh…ahhhh…my…" the man tried to say, but it seemed his jaw was…disconnected from the rest of him.

"Yeah, yeah, I hope I broke something real good, animal beater," Swoop said as he turned and walked toward the Gresham horses. The two animals almost seemed to smile at him. He strapped the Gresham saddle on either Classy or Sassy.

"You…you can't take…" the man said in a pained, garbled gasp.

"And yet, I am doing it as you speak."

Then he put a set of reins on their second horse. He mounted the saddled one, grabbed the reins of the second and trotted out the stall, headed for the stable's back doors, the prisoner wagon having been moved aside.

"Where do you think...you think you are going?" Deacon Williams arrived and asked, standing in the courtyard, stables doorway. He looked down at Anderson.

Swoop turned the horse around and guided Classy and Sassy near Williams. He tried to contain himself.

"I am going to a little place they call, 'Anywhere the fuck I want to'," Swoop said. And he so desired to dive off the horse and dismantle Williams into pieces, just from the angry look on Williams' face.

"You can't take those horses. Them horses ain't yours."

"These horses ain't yours either. They belong to a teenager I am about to go get," Swoop said.

He turned the horses, and they left the compound through the burned open stable doors. Up by the riverside road, he saw the trampled tracks of many horses and with the sun at a good angle creating slight shadows, within a minute, Swoop determined that whomsoever went after Luke Gresham, went east. Probably three horses. Then he spotted a pair of boot prints run in, out and under the trampled mess.

Swoop figured that Luke would either go west to try and catch up with the wagon train. Or he would go east, back to that last house where the residents told the wagoneers about the church and orphanage. It looked like the teen was bound back for that house, but to what end? For what?

"Let's go get yer boy," Swoop told Classy and Sassy, and off they went in a gallop.

Chapter 17: Ivan Lotsky, The Good Neighbor

"He's a free boy!" Ivan Lotsky yelled out to the three riders on his front yard.

Lotsky held a very old rifle, so decrepit it was unidentifiable to Ambrose, Svenson and Munday, as they sat on their horses about 20 feet from Lotsky's front porch.

"He say or tell you anything?" Ambrose asked.

"The boy said he felt like he was in a prison with y'all. About to be executed. Hung!"

"We are not a prison. We run a professional organization and there are rules to it," Ambrose said.

"Well, he won't go back."

"That is not possible. He is enrolled."

"En…enrolled? I don't understand," Lotsky said, "he needs a family to take care of him. He…enrolled… with you to find one and now he found one right here. So just consider him unenrolled with you. He's enrolled here. His sister too. I'm fixen' to get her. "

"That ain't the rules…of the, the church. Or the law."

"The law?" Lotsky said.

"The…law of orphans. Yeah. I want to talk with him."

"He does not want to talk with you."

"By God, he will, Lotsky! And that old piece a shit you call a rifle ain't gonna stop me. Us. It has a ridiculously long barrel. And it's single shot. I wouldn't use it for a fence post!"

Then they all heard thundering hooves. Swoop and the two horses left the river road and turned onto the rougher dirt road to the Lotsky house.

When close, Swoop slowed down, holding Randy's rifle in his right hand, the rifle butt resting on his right thigh. His two Thunderer holsters were not tied to his legs so the holsters' angle could rest straight up and down from the belt, for a faster draw when on horseback.

"What in all hells bells are you doing here?" Ambrose said.

Swoop ignored the remark and the three men.

"I want to talk with Luke," Swoop said.

"Like I told these fellers, he does not want to talk with anyone."

"You Mister Lotsky?" Swoop asked.

"Yes."

"Well Mister Lotsky, I need to talk with the boy."

"You with these church fellers?"

"No."

Swoop got off the horse and tied the reins of both animals to a small shrubby tree branch. He walked up to the house and Lotsky only moved his rifle up an inch or two, not aiming at him directly while looking at Swoop's big smile.

"I can straighten this out, sir," Swoop said, and walked

right past him and right into the house.

A woman and Luke sat at a dining room table near the front door, obviously in a bad state of nerves. The woman was squeezing a hand rag to death with both hands.

"Ma'am," Swoop said.

"The boy…" she started.

"I know."

He turned to Luke.

"What's going on here Luke? I am here to help you if I can."

"I left to get help. Get a sheriff or a marshal from somewhere. It's hell in that place."

Mrs. Lotsky winced at the curse word.

"Hell in what way, son."

"They…raped my sister."

"They did? They who?"

"That Williams guy and the guy named Anderson. They beat her. And they raped her."

"I know Williams, and I think Anderson is the one at the barn? The stables. Not sure," Swoop said.

"I am not sure, either. I think so."

"And that's how she got bruised?"

"Yes."

"Are you some kind of lawman?" Mrs. Lotsky asked.

"No ma'am. I can actually do better than that," Swoop said as an aside, still looking at Luke.

"We were there only a day, and Mister Last, and we knew. There's other girls there too. Some boys too. Raped. There's something really bad going on there. The kids that know are scared and won't say it out loud to you, but they told me."

"Not too sure you can stay here and be safe either, Luke. Let's go back, you and me. I'll take care of this rape thing and make sure Janet is safe. You aren't going to make it afoot to any city for any law. The law is days and days and miles away. Maybe I can fix some things up real quick? At least until you're sent to Spokane."

He stared at Swoop.

"I don't know what they got in mind for us in Spokane, Mister Last. It ain't no good either. Can't be. I left my sister to get some help. She'd only slow me down."

The woman started to cry.

"You know my story kid. I ain't one of them. I floated in here like a ghost. I'm leaving as soon as I can. Maybe you and your sister can come with me until we get to Spokane or somewhere. Somewhere else."

"What about all the other kids?" Luke said. "We can't leave them."

"Yeah. Yeah that's a point," Swoop admitted with a sigh. "I…maybe I can do something?"

"Like what?" Luke asked.

"Like…something."

Luke nodded and stood.

"Should I summon the law?" the woman said.

"No ma'am. I told you, I can do better and faster than the law. The law will get in my way."

She pursed her lips and nodded.

"Come on, I got Sassy and Classy outside. Can you ride real fast bareback?"

"Yes, sir I can."

"Good."

Luke and Swoop emerged from the house. Mr. Lotsky stepped aside to let them pass. Luke nodded at Mr. Lotsky.

"Thank you, sir," Swoop told the neighbor. "You did good. Best you could."

"Ha!" Svenson blurted out.

The trio were still on their horses.

Swoop saw that Munday had removed the reins from the tree branch and was now holding Classy and Sassy's reins. With Randy's rifle in his left hand, Swoop grunted and walked close. In less than a second, in a swoosh of leather, he drew his right-hand pistol out and up at Munday's face.

"No. Just no. Drop the reins or I will drop you dead right there where you sit."

"You wouldn't."

Swoop half smiled and said, "You think you are doing something here, stopping me, but you ain't. I ain't waiting."

"There's three of…" Ambrose started to say.

"Two in a second," Swoop said, still glaring at Munday's face. "And in another second, none of you at all. You dead first. "

Munday had seen this crazy man's merciless gunplay in action. His mind flashed back to the shooting of four Indians in about three seconds in front of the church. He grimaced and dropped the reins.

"We will be returning to the church, now. Which is what you wanted. Or half-wanted. If you try to pull some shit along the way? It won't work."

Swoop jumped on his horse and Luke barebacked the other. The duo busted off to the road and eastbound at a full gallop.

With a big lead and Swoop noted none of the three were bearing rifles to shoot them from a distance, they slowed down after a 5 minute run.

"That Ambrose," Luke said," He's wearing my dead uncle's gun and holster."

"I saw that. Yeah."

"They stole it from my chest."

"And there's a nun wearing your mother's bracelets."

"I don't know what to do," Luke said.

"Maybe I can figure something out."

"How can you protect us? All of us?"

"Don't know yet, kid."

"You could kill em' like you killed all the hinjins'."

"I could."

"That would solve it."

"It might, but it would be very hard. There's a lot of em."

Chapter 18: Swoop, the Bedeviled Doctor

The pair entered the stables and dismounted. The wounded stable deacon was in a chair, his chin held up to his head by a big white wrap. He could only mumble something between gritted teeth and Swoop passed him.

"I think I'll be right back," Swoop said, not looking at him.

They walked into the courtyard among some of the deacons, nuns, and orphans doing chores. They all stopped and watched. Janet included. Luke half-smiled at Janet, but also made an unsure expression, suggesting, "I don't know what will happen next." Given Swoop's reputation in the Indian battle, Luke anticipated something very big and bad was going to happen.

Swoop stopped by one Deacon.

"Williams." was all he said.

"Ah…eating," the Deacon innocently said and pointed.

Swoop nodded and turned for the mess hall. Then Luke waved at Janet to follow. Swoop handed Luke the rifle and his hat.

It was the last few minutes of breakfast, and the big room was less than half full. Swoop stopped and looked around. Williams was seated back to the wall, eating and talking with other men.

Swoop marched up to the table, planted his palms upon it and with one giant leap, swung both his legs up and right over the top of the table. Both his feet landed right on William's chest! The man and chair shot back to the wall, and he dropped off to the side. Swoop landed on his feet and kicked him several times as Williams, so shocked, crawled away, gasping

"What the…" the man cried out.

Swoop grabbed the man's jacket and though tearing it some, lifted the man onto his feet and tossed him right back over the next table onto the center floor. Then, in a chaos of food, plates, cutlery, cups, and scattering men, Swoop tipped the long heavy table over, right atop Williams. Swoop followed the table, stepping on its underside. With Williams pinned chest down under the table, his head and shoulders exposed, Swoop beat his face several times. Then he stepped off the table and yanked the man out from underneath while shaking him violently.

The stunned man tried to strike back wildly, but at this point, the angry monster in Swoop was impervious to pain. He stood the man up in the blurry volatility. He struck Williams with a full body, right-hand blow to the face.

"Don't fall!" Swoop demanded, following Williams stumbling backward,

Then a left blow.

"Don't fall…"

Then a right again.

"DON'T FALL!"

But Williams fell backward, knocked so far away by the third punch he fell down on his back.

"Get up! If you fall again, I can't beat you to death," Swoop roared in a strange hate-filled garble of growling sounds, hard for others to discern.

"You're already beating him to death!" Another deacon cried out.

This deacon came at Swoop from the side, trying to hit him. But Swoop backhanded-hammer-fisted his face with a left-hand, then hit his face again with a right fist in a powerful, lightning fast, one-two punch. That man was unconscious before he hit the floor.

Swoop returned to the babbling Williams. Grabbed him and stood him up again, but the man could not stand. He fell against a table and onto a clutter of chairs, all tumbling over.

"Can you hear me?" Swoop asked. He leaned in close, "Can you understand me?"

Williams' bloody eyes were wide. A tooth popped out of his mouth as he coughed. It landed and stuck right on Swoop's cheek. Didn't matter. Swoop expected stuff like that when he beat the guts out of a man.

"If you touch another kid, you hurt that girl again? I will cut shit off of you, while you watch me do it. You will live! You'll be an amputee living in a wheel barrel."

"Okay. Okay!" Father Penance said, having witnessed the whole harrowing event. He approached. "Okay, Charles. Charles! It's over." He courageously patted Swoop's shoulder and then started to grab it and slowly pull him away.

"That goes for every son of a bitch in here!" Swoop roared with spit and slobber flying out of his mouth, "nuns, priests, deacons, whatever in Hell you are!"

Swoop stepped back and Williams fell the rest of the way through the chairs to the floor. Swoop pointed his finger at Penance, then at Williams, then at Janet Gresham. For a moment, his rage was such, he could not speak. Then he said.

"He raped that girl," Swoop said.

Penance was quiet.

"So did Anderson. Where is he? Is he the guy at the barn?"

"He's in the stable. Yes," Penance said, "he works in

the stable. You…you, now just a minute. Wait! You already broke his jaw this morning.”

“The donkey-beater,” Swoop said in a slow growl.

Swoop turned to the door.

“You can’t shoot him!” Penance cried out. “You already beat him. You disconnected his jaw! Don’t shoot him!”

“I ain’t shootin’. Shootin’ is too fast,” Swoop growled.

On his way out, he saw Luke and Janet. The corner of his mouth twitched at them as he passed. He marched to the stables, and the others, all shocked, both orphans and employees forgetting and foregoing all rules, could not help but follow behind him.

Once inside the open barn door frame, Swoop spotted Anderson on a horse, off in the distance, galloping away in a cloud of dust from the compound. Swoop just stood there watching him, fists clenching and unclenching, catching his breath.

"Yeah. Yeah you ride away, You chicken-shit, piece-of-shit, muther-fucker. And you don't come back," he whispered.

When he turned, he saw Father Penance and others glaring at him in the courtyard. He stopped and eyed them all up.

"If any of these kids get hurt again," he said, calming down, " I will start killing people around here. You hear me? You hear me! I…will…kill…you!"

"You don't run this place," a deacon dared to say in a shaky voice.

"You! You brought all those heatherns here that damn near kilt' all of us, in the first place. They's a huntin' you!" another shouted.

"That's about right," Swoop said, "I don't run this place. I brought those indians here. Yeah. I am *NOTHIN* but trouble. I'm a lit stick of fucking dynamite. A got-damn whirlwind dervish. And you all stay the hell away from me and you stay away from hurtin' these kids!"

Behind the onlookers, two nuns and a deacon carried the limp Williams off to the staff rooms. He looked dead in their arms. It took three of them.

He walked up to Father Penance and asked," When do these kids leave for Spokane?"

"In two days, the Stringer Brothers are coming to pick them up."

"I'll be here that long. Then I am gone too. If you want any peace around here for two days? You'll leave me and these orphans alone."

With that Swoop left for the mess hall. He was suddenly really hungry. Inside, the nuns were cleaning up the smashing mess he'd made earlier. They were yelling at some of the kids to help, but got quiet when Swoop walked in. They didn't dare look at him. He collected some food on a plate, grabbed a cup of coffee and sat at one of the remaining, standing upright tables. He put a

Thunderer out and laid it up on the tabletop and ate. Luke walked in and placed the rifle and the hat on the table by him.

"You did do something Mister Last," the teen said.

No sooner did Swoop drop out of sight and into the mess hall, Ambrose, Munday and Svenson trotted into the stables and dismounted.

"Where's Anderson?" Munday wondered.

"Who knows. Probably getting coffee," Ambrose said.

"The twins' horses are back here. Last did bring Luke back like he said he would," Svenson said.

Ambrose shook his head and said, "At very least…."

"We need a meeting! Now!" Father Penance said as he appeared near a front stall. "Right now. Come on into my office. Hells broken loose."

Ambrose's eyes widened as he hadn't seen Penance act this commandingly and excited before.

Minutes later in Penance's office…

"He did what?" Ambrose said, "He did that to Williams?"

"He did," Father Penance told the three. "Over the rape of that girl twin."

Ambrose rubbed his head.

"Ve need to kill him," Svenson said.

"That's not so easy," Penance said. "You know he'll kill you in a second if you wink wrong at him. The man is a monstrosity. A demon. We all know this. We've seen him in action. He kills people like he's shootin at paper targets."

"I don't believe in demons," Svenson added, "neither do you."

"I do now," Penance confessed.

"Ve have to shoot him. Vhile he's asleep or some-zing."

Ambrose sat quietly.

"He looked me dead in the eye and said he was leaving in two days, after the orphans leave. Look, we don't want this kind of trouble for now," Penance said. "The Springer brothers and their friends will be here tomorrow. We can make the kid's move out in the middle of the night, while Last is asleep. We'll wake the kids up early. Get them in the wagons. He'll wake up the next morning and they'll be gone. He just told me that when the kids go, he'll go. He wants to go."

"He ain't no prospector like he said, no," Ambrose said.

"Something mighty mysterious happened out there in the desert. He's…he's a…a…"

"A devil," Penance said.

"Well, he acts like he's a Jesus," Munday said.

"Devil or Jesus, I think we could just give him a horse and even a little money and he'll leave, with all the brats already gone and we got our money," Ambrose said. "He'll leave thinking this is still a church and still an orphanage. Badly run maybe," he chuckled, "some criminals here, yeah, a crime or two here, yeah, but still a church and an orphanage, nonetheless. We have to keep this image up, ya know?"

"Yeah, let the Stringers have a good head start first," Munday agreed, "so if Last wakes up and leaves the next morning, he won't catch up to them."

"Where'd he say he'd go?" Ambrose asked.

"He didn't say," Penance said.

"Ven the Stringers get here and they hear vat happened, they vill vant to move in and kill him. We should just kill him now," Svenson said.

"That'll…hmmm…I don't know. More gunshots the kids might hear. And then they don't see Last around…" Penance wondered.

"No gunshots! You…you stab him. That is what you do. Stab him in the throat," Svenson said.

"Woulda, shoulda, coulda," Munday said with a moan. "I ain't going near him. He was about to shoot me dead back at Lotsky's front yard. I could tell I was nothing to him. His dang eyes cut right through me. I could tell he wanted to shoot me for holding them horse reins. His eyes! He was getting excited, even happy, about the idea."

"*Jag Kan Inte tro har!* All this playing around because of this one man? Charles Last?" Svenson said in a yell. "I say ve just kill him. Slit his throat. Knock him in the head and slit his throat and wrists. No gunshots."

"…and this Last goes missing? That'll just rile all the kids up," Penance continued. "Look, right now, I tell you, Last is a hero to these kids."

"I don't care if these kids get riled up? Who cares? They are like cattle to be rounded up and shipped off," Sven said.

Munday said, "No Sven. I guess we can play those two days out. Maybe with that twin girl raped, and Last being her hero, her savior, their dad-gum hero, maybe that might quiet the kids all down and be a good card for us to play. Just *two* days of…"

"Of peace," Penance said.

"Of peace. Yeah. Kids quiet with feeling a little hope thanks to this lunatic Last. Maybe the rape was a good thing in the end. Huh? Yeah," Munday said.

"It's not a good thing to Willams and Anderson," Penance said. "I will never let strangers in here to stay again."

"Now look, we have let strangers stay here before for a day or two," Ambrose corrected, "and we fooled them. We've fooled visitors before. We know how to do it. It helps for business to have good stories about us way out here."

"This is not one of those good stories," Svenson said. "He did save our lives, but he brought the Indians here to begin vith."

"Well Sven," Penance said, "those renegade Indians

would have come anyway, looking for us. You heard that Nerto wanted to take all the women and the food. Start a tribe. And you well know, they come around here every two years or so reeking of trouble. I say, keep the peace. It's just tonight and a day. And tomorrow night they leave after midnight," Penance summarized, looking at each of their faces.

Ambrose's right knee started moving side to side, his head up and down and he said, "Yeah. Everybody goes quietly. Munday, tomorrow you go east a ways, set up a little campsite for yourself on the river road. Wait there. Meet the Springers coming in. Tell them this story, this whole story about what's happened and all. Leave their wagons behind in Belittle's Cove. You all ride in, come on in to eat and sleep. Leave a man out by the wagons. Then after midnight, after Last goes to sleep, we go out and bring the wagons in well after midnight on the west side, outside the stable. We'll wake the kids up, line them up, shush' em up because the nuns are asleep, and get them out of here."

"Okay. Okay. Have our girls keep Last away from the orphans the rest of today and tomorrow – just say it's the rules – and we can wait it out," Penance said.

"Will Anderson ever come back?" Munday asked.

"He fled," Penance said, "Like David fled from Saul in the Bible. Broken jaw and all. When he heard Last knew about the rape of that Gresham girl, ooooh, Anderson fled. That loose jaw must have hurt bouncing away on a horse like that."

"Jaw? What exactly happened there with Anderson?" Ambrose asked.

"Last caught Anderson punching a donkey this morning in the stable."

"A...donkey?" Ambrose said. "Punching a donkey and..."

"Yes. Last saw him do it, roughed him out and threatened him.”

“Fer hittin’ a donkey?”

“Yes. Last hit him in the face with Randy’s rifle. Broke his jaw. Broke his face up badly. Sister Bloodworth ran to the barn while Last was beating Williams up in the cafeteria over the rape. She told him that Last would be after him next.”

“She knew about the rape? About Williams AND Anderson?” Ambrose said.

“She did, yeah,” Munday said solemnly, “she…she watched them rape the girl. She brought the girl into the barn. You know how Bloodworth is. Gets. About them young girls.”

Penance shook his head at that news. “Ohhh, dear God. I knew, I just knew this can’t go on. That this nonsense would catch up with us here.”

“You should lecture, preacher?” Ambrose said. “After all that you have done in New Mexico. You should lecture us? Lecture Anderson and Williams? And Bloodworth.”

Father Penance rubbed his face and head with both his hands, almost massaging his scalp.

“Yeah,” Ambrose said, always impatient with any goodness Penance might display.

“And they had to carry Williams to his bed,” Penance said between his palms. “It’s a wonder he’s still alive. He may die in bed.”

“That bad. That’s something,” Munday said. “He that bad?”

“I tell you, I have never seen a grown man beaten like this,” Penance continued, his hands now free of his head. “Like Williams was run over by a buffalo. And I have seen some church beatings and inquisitions down in the southwest. Torture, but slow torture. This Charles Last? He can… go… crazy. Throwing Willams and furniture around. He beat Williams like a bedeviled doctor would, knowing just exactly how and where to beat somebody up."

"Hmmm. Okay. Okay. Peace and quiet then for two days. That's the plan," Ambrose said. "Rest of today and one more day. Ignore Last. Keep him away from the kids."

Svenson shook his head, harboring…other plans. Deadly ones.

Chapter 19: Calico Reems, the Colonel and Marshal

Waters of the Pacific Northwest…

Three armed men in raincoats walked to the inlets edge, being lightly sprayed by the waving mists of the Pacific Northwest Ocean. They needed no torch to light the path to their 25-foot sailboat, the one they'd hauled up on the green and rocky coast the previous night. They pushed the boat out a bit and jumped in.

It was just another night of being…prey. Prey for pirates. They set up the three sails and drifted off, under the skippering of Wells Fargo agent Rory Pickles. Rory was the son of a professional fisherman from Lake Erie and Pickles knew a boat from stem to stern. Then at 18 he joined the U.S. Army where he served for 21 years, mostly under the command of one Colonel Calico Reems – now the Wells Fargo team leader and the man in the boat with him who sat right down on the deck in the stern, next to a pile of empty wooden boxes. Reems laid his double-barreled shotgun across his lap, fixing the sling for comfort. Wells Fargo agent Quinton "Canary" Dew untied the dock ropes that would secure the craft to shore should the tide rise unexpectedly from a storm and try to carry it off. Canary hailed from southern Alabama and also served 10 Army years under Colonel Calico Reems. Colonel Reems once nicknamed Dew "Canary" because on various military missions, Dew could spot and predict trouble like a warlock seer. Reems said that Dew was like "a canary in a coal mine," when sensing danger.

"Oh, and those canaries in the coal mines, Colonel? They die first," Dew reminded Reems frequently.

It helped that Canary was also a good long distance shot and a burly bruiser.

The empty boxes strewn about the deck were staged to look like a supply boat to lure out the area pirates. One trip they sailed south to Seattle or Portland and the next night they returned north to Alaska, all in hopes they would attract the burgeoning collection of waterway bandits. Retired U.S. Army Colonel, also U.S. Marshal and finally Wells Fargo chief detective Calico Reems, once stationed beside some boxes, pulled a cover over himself to completely disappear under the tarp.

As a result of his distinguished career, Reems had many government connections and five years earlier a troubled Arkansas Congressman Jacob Wallerwack handed Reems a Federal Marshal's badge in hopes the veteran might handle a Fort Smith problem requiring multi-state jurisdiction. Reems took the badge and turned it over and over in his hand, contemplating the responsibilities of such. He accepted and solved the congressman's problems. Wallerwack ensured that Reems remained a marshal ever since. This additional, handy responsibility was beloved by Wells Fargo! Reems could roam the country on Wells Fargo assignments and also command federal police authority.

This night, as the nights before, and probably many more to come, U.S. Marshal and Wells Fargo agent Reems looked like part of the vessel's supplies under a tarp.

"Night, night, Colonel," Canary said sarcastically.

"Wake me when the war's over," Reems said. Then he cursed at his undercover predicament, even though he would expose his head from time to time and talk with his two old, tough compatriots.

Canary and Pickles could not discern the exact muffled curse from under the thick cover. At least the Colonel would remain dry tonight. Two oil lamps, aglow hung on each side of the craft, burned into the night. They also served as an outline of the boat, an easy-to-spot enticement for pirates. Like moths to the flame,

The trio were but a tiny part of a commerce war between Seattle, Washington, Tacoma, Washington and Portland, Oregon, a struggle over shipping superiority. Portland had an advantage in population and sailable, related inland waterways to send far eastern and western coast products back East. But the business leaders in Seattle were determined to dominate the markets over other nearby coastal cities.

The various big and small gold rushes in Alaska brought much northwest ocean passage business to those states and Canada. This included supplies and hopeful people sailing north. Gold, and successes and disappointments of those coming back south kept the waterways busy. All this transportation came in a variety of steamships, sailboats, smaller sail boats and even row boats that clung to the coastlines trying to avoid travel expenses and the testy trials of the open seas.

The dreams and realities of gold diggers and their support systems spawned hijacking problems via all these waterways. They brought forth a new form of piracy, thievery and…even stealing boats. Pirate boats of various sizes were appearing day and night from the inlets and ramming or stopping smaller supply lines under the threat of gun barrels. And as criminals are wont to do, many got more confident and outrageous with each successful crime. The pirates started kidnapping, even killing some of the sailors and passengers, shooting them or casting them overboard to drown. The stolen boats would then be used for even more piracy hijackings, and also re-sold in a new black market of needy prospectors and businesses (probably to eventually be re-stolen back to the pirates in a cycle).

U.S. Customs Revenue cutter ships patrolled the Northwest coast too, but with bigger missions in mind to supply lighthouses and stop international smuggling from Canada and the Far East with a goal of just collecting taxes and tariffs. For them hijacking, piracy and murder of the smaller boats of the working man was not a priority.

Seeking a professional, organized response, a frustrated Yukon Outfitters hired Wells Fargo to investigate the problem. The home office shipped Reems and his two partners northwest to crack the problem.

Reems considered the crimes much like stagecoach robberies, except over the water. But after 4 months and after much fruitless, spot-searching the lengthy, seemingly endless, ragged and jagged coastline, which was over some 2,000 miles, they could only collect the sad tales of victims. To their estimation, there must have been a thousand wicked little places of concealment from which pirates could launch their raids.

Thwarted, Colonel Reems decided their best and only hope was to sail north and south near the shoreline in a small fake supply ship or a prospector's craft and draw some pirates out after them. He convinced Yukon Outfitters, now very impatient and demanding some results, to give them a boat for this experiment. Reems felt as though, if he could prove his point, a small fleet of private patrol boats and steamship-motherships would be needed to protect the coast. They would have to speckle the waters with "victim" boats to seduce the thieves and murderers out into ambushes.

Their 15th night on the water was underway for several hours. True to his nickname, Canary's head snapped to the left. He shielded his eyes from their lamps with his hands.

"Something…" he whispered.

Pickles walked to the rear.

"Colonel? You awake, boss?"

"I heard," Reems said. "Keep me posted, boys."

The encroaching boat turned south a few degrees, apparently in an effort to intercept. The craft drew closer and closer.

"Colonel, this boat," Canary started, "it's got itself a metal front for ramming. It…it looks like a rigged-up war wagon. At least a 40-footer."

"Damn Vikings! How many people?"

"I think four," Pickles said.

The rammer got within shouting distance.

Then it started, a "Viking" lifted a pistol to the night sky and fired, cracking open the quiet coast with a flash of light and sound.

"They shooting at us?" Reems asked.

"Not yet. They killed a cloud."

"Ahoy, you over there!" the shooter yelled out.

"What say?" Pickles yelled back.

"You drop those sails! You drop em er you die right here, right now sailor scum!"

Pickles began lowering the sails. Under the canvass, Reems cocked back both barrels of his shotgun.

"That's a good little boy!"

Then Pickles and Canary stood up, hands in the air.

The pirate craft maneuvered side-to-side with their

boat. Three men with rifles had their beads on the two. Their fourth man ran their ship and sails like a master seaman.

"What chu boys got yonder in those boxes? They ain't fill of gold, are they?"

"No sir. No. Just supplies," Canary said, trying to hide his anger within a scared, shaky voice. Just inside his coat pocket, barrel down was a 6 shot, short, barreled revolver. The same armament existed in Pickles' pocket.

One man lowered his rifle and quick tied the crafts together. Two of them stepped over onto their boat, handling the wave rocking like experts.

"Coming aboard, are ya?" Pickles shouted, so that Reems would know.

"Of course, we are, why else are we here? What's under this here big tarp?" One pirate asked, walking astern.

The man stepped over, checking his balance against the choppy water and reached for the tarp's edge. The second man looked eagerly toward the tarp, his gun barrel still close and aimed at Pickles, just not looking at him. Canary and Pickles readied themselves for instant trouble.

The curious man pulled back the tarp in a single fling…and Reems shot him square in the chest with a single barrel blast. It was so close, the whole round barely spread and smacked him hard like a slug. This man dropped his rifle and flew back and down.

Pickles yanked the other man's gun barrel aside that was aimed at him and smashed that man in the face with the bottom side if his fist. The man fell, leaving the rifle in Pickles' hand. Pickles got a proper two-hand-hold on the long gun and struck him in the face with the barrel. He too fell.

Meanwhile, Canary dropped, drew his pocket pistol and shot the rifled man on the other boat. He stumbled back wounded, still standing for just a second as Reems stood up and hit him with the second round of the scatter gun. That shot had the distance to scatter, tearing up the man's chest and neck and peppering the wooden cabin and rail around him, Reems dropped the empty double barrel shotgun to the end of it's sling, and pulled his pistol.

The fourth man on the pirate ship raised his hands.

"I am just a sailor. A sailor man. I'm no gunman," he shouted pitifully.

"Well then just-a-sailor man," Reems declared, "come forth and step on over here."

The man did, using his hands for balance as little as possible, trying to keep those palms-up, held up high.

When aboard, Canary searched him, then shook his head at Reems. No guns or knives.

"Sit," Reems ordered.

The other struck man started mumbling and groaning. Reems lifted his shotgun from the end of its sling and put two more buckshot rounds in it.

"Who are you?" Reems asked the sailor.

"My name is Bertram Goebbels. I…"

"They hire you to set sail these boats?" Reems said.

"Yes, they did. They do.."

"You Dutch? You sound Dutch."

"Yes, ah. I am German."

"Uh-Huh. How long you been doing this?"

"You don't say shit!" the other man down on the deck warned, coming more around to his senses from the prior strike to his head.

"And who then are you?" Reems said, walking over to the prone, stunned man.

"You may as well give me a name. I ain't a telling," the criminal said.

"Uh huh," Reems said.

"That's right."

"Where's your port? Your headquarters?" Reems asked.

"You may as well make one up. I ain't a telling."

"Uh-huh. I may as well blow one of your feet right off then."

The man didn't know or have time to say something. Canary and Pickles snatched him up, put his rear end on a box and hung the lower half of his left leg over the edge of the boat. Canary had him by the throat with one hand and an arm with the other hand.

Reems walked up and aimed his shotgun at the man's ankle and foot, inches away, and smiled.

"Thanks, boys. Because you know, I don't want to blow a hole in the boat."

"No…NOOOO!" the man mumbled between Canary's fingers and palm.

"I will blow your left foot off…"

Canary let go of his face so he could talk.

"I'll tell you!" the German sailor yelled out from the left to interrupt the act of maiming.

"I ain't talking to you, Dutch!" Reems said, without looking back at him.

"B...B…Billy!" came a garbled, strained voice from the other boat!

That third rifleman that was just pistol shot by Canary and buckshot by Reems from a distance a moment earlier was still alive over there! Bloody fingers wrapped the gunwale – the side of the boat - and half of his bloody face slowly appeared.   The eyes were wide with the expression of pain and shock. He looked like a monster that half-ate someone bloody and raw.

Reems spun, and shot him again, and the exposed part of the face ripped away like in a blurry, gale force.

"Gimlet!" The held man screamed out.

"That's enough of Mister Gimlet then," Reems said. "Now. About… this… here foot," Reems continued. "You want to limp around the rest of your life on a peg? Or what?"

And he placed the end of the shotgun back inches from the man's ankle. "Maybe we'll do both feet and give you a matching set? You'll crawl on the floor or on the mud just to eat dinner or take a shit. Rest of your whole life. Footless. Footless just fer being dang fool stupid for a few minutes right here and now."

"Alright, alright, I'll tell ya. I'll…I'll show ya. It's Chesterville Cove. There's cabins there and they use a cabin, like an office," the man said, panting from shock.

Canary reached for a metal box and produced two pairs of shackles.

"Cuff Dutch around front. We need him to sail that boat," Reems said. "Cuff this son of a bitch here around back. We need for him to worry about drowning in case I toss him overboard." He leaned into the man. "I'll take no guff from you, mister sister."

"They'll be no guff from me no more," the man said reluctantly.

"What's your name in case I have to fill out a death certificate?"

"Brent Maloney."

"Where from?"

"Peachtree County, Georgia. Ain't no city yet where I'm from."

"Uh-huh. Long way from home, Mister Maloney. Shoulda stayed there. Who's this other dead bastard over there?" And Reems pointed at the gut-shot, dead man in the stern of the boat, the one he'd first blasted when his tarp was lifted.

"Belladado. Don't know his first name. He's from Italy."

"Italy! Another idiot from afar. And that dude I just shot in the other boat?"

"Reggie Gimlet."

"From?"

"Vancouver," Brent Maloney said.

"Canadian. Eye-talian, German and a Peachtree," Reems said, watching Canary do all the handcuffing. "That's a wild hand of cards."

When the cuffing was complete, Reems stood the German up.

"You and my man here will sail to Seattle. We'll follow. Then we will get some more men and you will take us to your dock at Chesterville Cove tomorrow morning."

"I…" the German said.

"I, what?" Reems said.

"Yes sir," the German said.

"How many pirates are there? How many boats?"

"They will come in and out all night. Sometimes with boats, sometimes with stolen goods. Sometimes with kidnapped people," Bertram Goebbels confessed.

"Kidnaped?"

"Yes. They take some people for ransom."

"That ever work?" Reems asked.

"Sometimes."

"If it doesn't?"

"They…they just kill them. They got a woman and a man tied up there now. A little boy too. About half dead. No food. No water."

"Again, how many pirates?" Reems asked.

"Tonight? Maybe 20," Goebbels said.

Reems reached under his big hat, scratched his head, and thought about that.

"What do they do in the daytime?"

"They sleep. They eat. Play cards. Sometimes they go to Seattle."

"Twenty of em, you say?"

"Ja."

"That a yes in Dutch?"

"Yes."

"Who's in charge? Who is the top boss?" Reems asked.

"I don't know his full name, his real name. They call him Rembrandt."

"Know where he's from?"

"Los Angeles. California."

"Okay then," and he turned to Maloney. "Mister Maloney, you lay down right here, face down."

Maloney did, and with a nod of Reems' head, Canary guided Bertram Goebbels over to the next boat and helped him set up the sails for the ride to Seattle. Pickles set up their sails. Reems looked at his pocket watch. It would take an hour or so to get to Seattle and it was only 9 p.m.

"What we gonna do, Colonel?" Pickles asked Reems.

"I don't think we get 20 marshals or deputies to make this run tonight. We might take the Dutch sailor back in the morning with enough men. Twenty scoundrels the likes of these gun-happy suckers are too much for us to handle alone."

"Yes, sir."

"And I do worry about those kidnapped people, but they will have to hang on till morning."

"Yes, sir."

"Colonel!" Canary shouted.

Reems looked over at him on the other boat.

"Dynamite," Canary said holding up a stick and standing by the cabin.

"Huh?" Reems said.

Reems walked near Maloney, now handcuffed and prone on the deck.

"Peachtree! What do you boys do with dynamite?"

"Sometimes we decide that we need to blow up a boat. Maybe we've made a mess of things, and we'll just sink the boat," the facedown, crook said, his mouth scrunched into by the wooden deck.

"Sometimes people on board?" Reems asked.

"Well…yeah well, sometimes," Maloney said.

"They die?"

"I…I reckon they die."

"Uh-huh," Reems said.

The two boats coasted into a downtown, busy boat dock at 10:10 p.m. Reems jumped out first, dodged some oily rats, and jogged to the dockmasters office up on the paved street.

"US Marshal," Reems said, showing his badge to the employee in the office booth window. "What is the fastest way to get the city police or the Marshal's office here."

"Take this whistle, Marshal." The clerk said, "that next block right there is Main Street. Get down there and blow and blow the whistle. There are usually police walking there on Main Street. They'll come a running and they have crank a phone call box on some street light poles around here. They'll call for help. Is there anything I can do?"

Reems took the whistle, "You just did, sir."

"I'll be needing that there whistle back, sir."

"And you'll get it back, sir."

Reems followed the clerk's orders, attracting quite a bit of attention from the natives and tourists in this commercial area. And from among them, two patrolmen came running as predicted. Reems showed his badge and explained his situation. They led him over to a metal light pole and with a skeleton key, one opened a metal box on the pole. Inside was a phone and one officer commenced cranking and calling.

Reems brought the whistle back to the dock office, and helped Canary and Pickles make Goebbels and Maloney pull the two bodies from the boats. They dropped the dragged corpses on the street right in front of the dockmaster, whose eyes about popped out of his head at the sight of the dead. Pickles ordered the two suspects to sit down on the ground.

Within a few minutes, the officer left the phone box and

reported back, "The Marshals office said they know you. They have the best jurisdiction for this, but my dispatcher will also tell the county sheriff too. We told them you had two prisoners. They'll meet you here, in a lickety-split, with a prisoner paddy wagon, Marshal."

"Thanks boys."

"You shoot these fellers?" The officer asked.

"Shot em dead. Trying to kill me," Reems said.

"That will be looked at by the Marshals and the County," the officer said. "All that is out of our jurisdiction. We'll be taking our leave."

The two city patrolmen left.

In some thirty minutes, two U.S. Marshals arrived in a small coach, and introducing themselves as Galahad and Peconte. Then a plain-clothes, county deputy named Periwin showed up on horseback. The three listened to Reems explain his predicament.

"I think it best that we go tomorrow morning as these scalawags might be asleep by then," Reems summarized.

"We've got two small schooners yonder," Marshal Galahad said pointing out to the docks. "We can take one with you to the Cove."

"We ain't got no boats here," County Deputy Periwin advised, "but we can send a wagon to Chesterville Cove. It'll take longer."

"How much longer?" Reems asked.

"About two hours by land. It be a little rugged up yonder, Marshal. Rocky roads and all the way down to the Cove off the main road, but you'll need land transport anyway fer' the prisoners. We can help them kidnapped people too. I'll take these two to the jail."

"We'll need the Dutch sailor to guide us in the morning."

"You'll get em. I'll have someone bring em. The sheriff office needs a head start on the wagon in the morning."

"I reckon we'll leave from here at 8:30. That enough

time for you boys to get a head start?"

"Yessir."

"We'll leave from here since our boat and their boat is here," he pointed the two marshals. I would like to sail in on their boat. It has quite a metal rig up front for ramming and maybe they'll see her come in and think little of it till we get really close."

The men all nodded.

"I like it," Reems said. "Let's say we hit the camp from the road in and the coast both at 9:30. What say ye?"

"You boys land right at the Cove," Marshal Galahad said. We'll coast in and stop a bit away. Land her and sneak in from the side."

"And we'll hit it from the back road," the deputy said.

"That's a 3-sided assault. Remember we can't get in a crossfire. Can you fellers sail?" Reems asked the Marshals.

"Like a goldarned fish," Peconte said.

"Eight-thirty a.m. then? Here?" Reems said.

"Yes sir. We'll have about 10 men," Galahad said.

"We'll have us 2," Periwin said. "I'll call the funeral home for these two chumps. Leave em here. Their meat wagon will come and get em."

"And charge these two scoundrels with attempted murder of a federal officer," Reems told Periwin. "That'll be me! We'll sort the mess out tomorrow."

"My whole life has turned out to be no good," Maloney leaned over and told Goebbels.

Pickles and Canary walked over to the suspects. Pickles removed their shackles and Deputy Periwin cuffed the men with his handcuffs.

"We'll ride over to the jail with you," Galahad told Periwin.

"Thanks, Gal," the deputy said.

Reems walked up to the dockmaster shack.

"Mister Dockmaster," Reems told the man through the window, "thank you for your whistle and your help. Now…

where is the closest Inn?"

"Two blocks East, yonder. Ahh, you gonna…you gonna leave those two dead fellers right there? It's bad for business!"

"I'll say," Reems said.

"Can ya at least cover their faces with hats?"

"They didn't come with no hats," Reems said. He winked and the three Wells Fargo agents left.

At 8:30 a.m. A deputy delivered Geobbels at the dock as promised. He reported that the wagon posse had left earlier and was in route to the cabins. The two Marshals were ready to set sail in their schooner.

Pickles, Canary, Reems and Geobbels stepped aboard the "pirate" ship. Geobbels prepped the sails. Pickles undid the lines and off they went.

In fair winds, the two boats left for the North. Bound for Chesterville Cove, The German sailor, Reems, Pickles and Canary in the pirate vessel, followed by the two Marshals in their boat.

"Vhat vill become of me?" Goebbels asked Reems, wiping the cold sea spray from his face.

"Well sir, you're a pirate. A picaroon. An accomplice. I don't rightly know what will become of you, but helping us out here and now, will help you later. I'll speak for you."

"If I can come out of this alive," Goebbels said shaking his head side to side. "These men are crazy. I think this is going to be terrible. Like a var. Shoosting'. I left Germany because of the little vars vit neighbor countries."

"Europe problems. America problems. I know a Chinese man in Seattle who likes to say, 'same-same,'" Reems said."And America and Europe? Same-same. Are you involved with using the dynamite aboard on other boats?"

He was quiet, then confessed, "Yes. I mean, I did not light and throw these explosive sticks, but I saw the men that did."

"And some people died?"

"Some did, yes. I am sure."

Reems sighed and just looked ahead. Knowing those boats and missing people are all lost at sea. This ambiguity led to his decision to be ambiguous about who he shot and killed.

As they drew near the docks of Chesterville Cove, the three dropped down out of sight, below the craft's gunwales, leaving only Goebbels to remain standing and in view. Behind them the Marshal's little craft turned for shore, to disembark and advance on foot. One Marshal waved at Canary and Canary saluted back.

"The Marshal have cut off," Canary said.

"Understand," Reems said.

"See anybody?" Rory Pickles asked Goebbels.

"Some. Not many."

Goebbels worked the sails, slowing the boat down, steering toward the dock.

"No other boats. That's odd," Goebbels said. "Oh, they are over there." He pointed to the left to a small, side dock. Many of the boats were pulled up halfway on land.

"Ahoy, there Dutch!" suddenly came a distant, male voice. "Where's ya bloody crew?"

And Dutch Goebbels did not know what to say.

"They stole a boat and will be coming shortly," Reems whispered.

"They stole a boat and vill be coming shortly," Goebbels hollered.

Silence.

"They knoooow…they know," Goebbels said in a worried whisper, suddenly stricken with even more fear.

And that was the last thing Goebbels ever said. With a thump and a splatter, he was shot in the chest with a rifle round. Goebbels fell straight back, dead, his head hitting the wooden deck like a melon. He landed next to Reems, his lifeless eyes wide open until someone cared to close them.

The three agents were expecting troubles, but not this soon and were still shocked. They dared not stand up or peek over the sides. They twisted their bodies to lie flat on the deck face up, guns out and at the ready. From the already encroaching momentum, the boat drifted closer to the docks.

Then came a lightning storm of flashes that they could see from a hail of explosions. Bullets from pistols, rifles and shotguns. It was devastating. Like a gauntlet. The enemies' apparent goal? Blow the sides of the craft into splintered smithereens and kill all aboard, and these rounds were slowly doing their job. But this vessel had that metal ramming front which slowed down some of the destruction.

The sailboat ever so slowly coasted in, taking the ballistic beating, and would soon be bound to bump into the docks in a few minutes. They were closing in and further under some surrounding, coastline trees of the inlet.

"Trees," Canary said, once again the great predictor of trouble.

"Three of em aboard!" A man above cried out while hanging from a branch.

This caused the trio of agents to raise their weapons skyward.

Reems spotted the man that yelled out. He was some 15 feet up on a thick branch. Catching him before this sniper could shoot down at them, Reems blasted him with both barrels of his shotgun. The man was shredded apart and could only gasp as he slipped off the branch and dropped into the water.

Pickles did the same from his side to some lofty enemy. This falling man however, half hit the side of the boat, then plopped dead in the water.

Meanwhile, the horizontal barrage continued its destruction on the sides, chipping away on the agent's cover. Concentrated fire blew a hole in the gunwale. Reems could see the landing right through it.

"This is becoming 'Charon's Skiff of the Dead!'" Reems said, and the men shoulder-walked back from the stern and away from the new hole.

"Where's the cavalry?" Pickles said.

"I thought we were the cavalry!" Canary said.

Pickles was too busy to comment further. He'd had wormed his way, shoulder-walked, to the half-open, exposed cabin, and Reems and Canary thought that distancing and extra cover was a good plan. But Pickles had another mission in mind. Once inside the recessed area, he reached into that box of dynamite he'd found the day before. He pulled out a stick and plucked a box of matches from his coat pocket. Without fumbling, he lit a stick and like throwing a knife a long distance, with many flips, he flung that sizzling stick straight forward toward shore as hard as he could. As it blew in a shock wave of sound and force, he was lighting a second one and tossed it far to the left, and then lit a third and tossed it far to the right. Shortly after, they heard the sounds of moaning, and the angst of wounded men.

In these three, shock wave aftermaths, Reems thought it the time to take to a knee, peek over the side and see who or what was left. Some men were down, some were trying to stand to keep shooting.

"Where IS the other cavalry," Reems said aloud to himself.

There was a cavalry of sorts. The two support marshals had disembarked from their small watercraft. And about the time when the land firing commenced, the officers were crouched over, with rifles in their hands and dashing to the grounds area by the docks. They encroached behind a line of kneeling and prone pirates. They sized up what they could spy, then also laid prone and began shooting into the backs of the men, with a steady rage of gunfire. With their ears ringing from the dynamite, few criminals discerned that a steady barrage of shots rang out from their rear. The Marshals quickly shot down 8 enemies, before the ninth turned to look their way. That man tried to yell out about the ambush, but his warning was drowned out from the deafness of the dynamite bombardment, and then to be shot in the left temple.

Then the next cavalry of sorts arrived from the Sheriff's office. That wagon full of men turned onto the cabin grounds, almost tipping over from urgency. Six deputies bailed out of the open bed while firing, dropping even more bandits.

The remaining scoundrels began to see their friends fall in their peripheral vision, and they stopped shooting at the agents to look around, saving the boat from further attack. When the pelting of the boat ceased, the three Wells Fargo agents sat up and peered over the gunwale. The evil, now confused crew was north of them, and the deputies and marshals were to their right and east. The agents were free to fire at the pirates from their new flank.

The two-sided attack east and south was too much for the bandits, as the wounded or dead fell, and a handful scrambled to escape to the west. The agents jumped from the boat and the law enforcement officers finally con-verged. They cautiously approached the downed men.

"Give it up and toss your guns if you are among the living and if you wish to remain so!" a deputy declared.

Some pistols and rifles were tossed.

"Help me then!" a man cried out.

"We'll see about that!" another deputy said.

None of the officers were shot or even winged! Some moved to check on the five cabins on the grounds. The biggest and main one stood in the center.

Reems ran through and around the maudlin circle of bloody criminals and advanced to the main cabin. Several deputies joined him. Some of the deputies kicked the front door and burst inside. There was a single gunshot.

Reems arrived inside to see the police fussing on a man, a woman and boy tied up on the floor, looking worse for wear. And he saw a dead thug half propped up against a wall, face just about gone, legs straight out on the floor, the reason for that single gunshot. Most of his jaw landed in a windowsill in a blob beside him.

"Sheriff's Office ma'am. This catastrophe is now over," one said, untying her.

The recused woman and boy started to cry. The man seemed just about to.

Reems tipped his hat back with a finger flick on the brim. He stepped outside, nodded and winked at Pickles and Canary, who stood at the ready should there be more surprises. They understood the message that the kidnapped were alive, well and rescued.

"Marshal Reems?" one deputy approached him.

"Yes sir?"

"This telegram came in last night for you, from Wells Fargo."

"Oh? Ah, okay, thank you."

Reems took the envelope and unfolded the message inside. Curious, Canary and Pickles walked up to him.

"Ha! Hum!" Reem said shaking his head in some disgust.

"What Colonel?" Canary asked.

"Seems…seems they…well…you remember Lt. General Mordecai Swoop Swellen?"

"Of course," Canary said.

"Sure do boss," Pickles said, "hunted man now. He dead?"

"No. Not yet. Well…headquarters wants us to go east

and find him. They think maybe Swoop has killed five of our agents about two-three weeks ago. Somewhere on or near the Oregon Trail."

"Swoop?" Canary said, "killed…"

"Yeah," Reems said. "Man, I hate this."

"I hate this too," Pickles said. "I'd rather stay out of this with Swoop. Always liked him…"

"Me too," Canary said.

"And honestly, I'm about half scared to go up agin him," Pickles confessed. "He's a lunatic when provoked."

Reems sighed. His hand holding the telegram dropped to his side.

"Fraid, boys, we have to now," he said.

Chapter 20: Svenson and The Exploded Hand

Swoop spent most of the day in the mess hall and in a chair out in the courtyard. No one bothered him, not even Ambrose. Ambrose walked by him once and only winked and half-smiled, never even looking at Randy's rifle. Swoop knew something new was brewing against him.

His trips to the outhouse were worrisome, being in a closed wooden box unable to see any planned ambush developing outside. He considered walking off into the hillsides. When inside one, he laid a Thunderer on his bare thigh. But no troubles occurred. All the orphans looked and smiled at him now as they ate and did their chores. Swoop figured that if the deacons amassed an attack on him, in broad daylight, while he was inside an outhouse, the orphans might revolt!

Rosy the nun passed him a few times, and surreptitiously waved a low hand at him, which was a telltale sign that all the employees were ordered to stay away from him. Which to Swoop, was just fine.

Only young Foley Delane had the guts to approach him for a moment.

"Hello Foley Delane," Swoop said.

"Mister Last. You really beat up Deacon Williams for hurting Janet Gresham."

"I did."

"Why"

"Well like you said, he hurt Janet Gresham. He hurt her face and…he hurt her…insides too."

"Not sure the Bible would like that?"

"You are quite the reader, Foley Delane. First Edgar Allen Poe, now the Bible. I am not an expert on the Bible, but I do know it says many things. Says to do many things."

"There are some mighty big savings in that book."

"There are," Swoop said. "Big uns."

"You saving us, Mister Last?"

"I am saving you all until you can get to a better orphanage, I guess," Swoop said.

"Why?"

"You sure ask a lot of questions," Swoop said.

"Saving because you are a good, Bible man?"

"Some say I am, kid. Some say otherwise. I don't think about such things, being good or bad. I just sorta feel them out as they come and go."

"The nuns say you have a terrible temper. They say that's not good. Before my momma died, we memorized books, and the Bible too."

"How'd she die?"

"She fell in factory. Full of machines. She fell into the machines. They cut her up into pieces."

"Oh, I see. I am sorry, for her and for you."

"I don't see how I can ever be happy again, Mister Last."

"I...see. What about your paw?" Swoop asked.

"Never know'd him."

"I see."

"The Bible says that a hot-tempered man stirs up strife."

"Probably so kid," Swoop said, "two of those nuns are looking at us right now and you'd best run along before they put the wrath of God on you right now."

"They beat us with a paddle for almost nothin.' I think they like it."

"Yeah, they probably do."

Foley Delane didn't smile. He grimaced and just walked away.

Swoop watched the little man walk away, in many ways older than his years. Swoop gave the two nuns the evil eye, while he thought about a woman falling into mechanical, factory machines, whatever that means, whatever they were, and dying.

Dinner. Swoop sat down alone with a Mexican-based meal and a Thunderer pulled out and on the table. Father Penance carried his plate and cup over to sit next to him.

"Charles."

"Father. Looks like I caught a yellow fever around here."

"You have had a calm day?" the priest asked, almost smiling, "being left alone?"

"Left alone," Swoop said. "After whippin' Williams I have been. He recovering?"

"I believe so. Somewhat. He's in and out of sleep. Vomiting. He's missing teeth. The nuns found only one. We suspect that he swallowed the rest."

"Had one stuck on my cheek for a few minutes. Too bad for him. A sad rapist story," Swoop said, "I shouldna' killed him. Spared him the recovery. I'll bet there have been a lot of rapes here."

"You don't know that."

"Do you know that? I'll bet you know something. And you know Ambrose is walking around here with the twin's uncle's gun on his hip. And one nun, Bloodworth, is wearing their mother's bracelets."

"Charles, these men and women work here for almost nothing. Low pay. They…"

"…steal. And some get their pay from sex off of kids, I'll bet. Working for almost nothing. Finding homes for orphans is no excuse for screwing em' and stealing from them."

"What are you going to do?" Penance asked. "Take the gun and bracelets from them. Put them back in their storage chests? Beat up Ambrose and a nun too?"

"Maybe. Sounds like a plan. Righting some wrongs. Don't know yet. But it sounds like a dream idea to me."

"Why do you care?" Penance asked. "You are a prospector you say. Once in the Army. What is all this to you?"

"That's a good question. A kid asked me this same thing this morning. But why don't *you* care, Padre? You are the head priest here."

"I am not in charge here. These deacons…well…"

"They're not deacons. They're thugs. And best I can tell, these nuns ain't nuns either. I got one nun crawling all over me with her hand down my pants every time I stand still near her. There's some kind of racket going on here. Maybe you all are collecting some big money from a rich benefactor and doing a really bad, half-assed job with these kids?"

Father Penance did not answer. He just continued eating. Swoop stared at him.

"Ain't saying, are you?" Swoop said.

Silence.

"Well, I will be glad to get out of here. When the kids go west, I go east."

"We will be glad to see you go," he stopped eating and looked at Swoop, his patience at an end. "You have done nothing but cause trouble. You made Indians come here and try to kill us. You beat up two of our men, one almost to death. Now you say we are all criminals. If you must stay to watch over the orphans? Then fine. They will be gone maybe tomorrow or the day after tomorrow. The Stringer brothers will be here to pick them up and take them away. They'll be gone and we will give you some money and a good horse to…sweet Jesus Heaven above… just leave us alone after the orphans leave."

"The Stringer brothers. Well, I will be more than happy to oblige, Padre," Swoop said. "And yes, I have brought you all trouble. But there's plenty of trouble here already when I got here. And you have a piece of lettuce stuck on your cheek."

The priest wiped at it.

"The other side."

After dinner, Swoop retreated to his church bedroom with a jug of water and crackers in his pocket. Would a revenge ambush of some kind occur this night? Or would they just leave him be for one more night, one more day and night?

Now back in his room for the evening, he thought about his safety. In the military, if and when on hostile grounds, a leader sends out pickets - guards to watch the camp. But, when alone, you are the guard, the picket. He closed the window shutter and had a picketing idea. The metal bed-frame. He turned it sideways in the narrow room and it barely fit crossways. What if he pushed it up against the door? In this position, the room door, which opened inwards, would quickly hit the frame within a few inches. He shoved it into that position to see.

An intruder, pushing open the door and hitting the bed might make the bed move a bit across the floor and would be squeaky noisy. And it would make for a slow-down night attack. When he pushed the door up against the bed, an attacker would have to shove the bed away from the door just to get those few more inches of the door opening to get inside. A gun hand could enter a bit, but a shooter could not see Swoop if he were off to the right of the door. For more confusion, Swoop could pile the rickety room chair on top of the bed.

The chair would probably fall if the bed was shoved hard enough, causing even more a distraction.

He put the bed in place. He hauled the sad excuse for a mattress off from the bed and laid it on the floor for his sleep. He stood the chair up on the bed.

Hands on his hips, Swoop stared at his handiwork, satisfied that at least for that night, he had a bit of an alarm should a renegado deacon, deacons or nuns decide to sneak in and kill him.

Swoop sat on his floored mattress thinking. When could he leave this place? Two days? He had committed himself to these orphans, at least for a while. He had no money but for 6 stinking dollars from Adrian Glance. Father Penance offered him money to leave. No horse of his own, but the priest promised him a horse too if he'd leave. Some money and a horse.

And surely Wells Fargo would soon make the rounds looking for their missing men. Then how long before the Ditch Diggers bounty hunters catch wind of all this? Every day is like a ticking time bomb for him now more than ever. What if any, revenge, will the deacons meet out for him now that he has beaten two of them badly? He knew he would have to be his own guard now, be his own picket and post his lone self.

He thought about the land outside the compound. He recalled the land north, over the back wall. It rose steadily to a distant high mesa. He could sneak out and walk out there a ways off and sleep safer at night. He was a confirmed rambler these last two years as a fugitive and sleeping under the moon became a welcome habit. This was a plan for tomorrow night, his last night there.

He would still eat dinner and breakfast in the mess hall, his back against the wall and drop outside at night with the bed's blanket. Then he would find out exactly when these orphans would depart too. He was already told it would be soon. Two days? But soon wasn't soon enough. At this point the church people would be more than glad to see him go, if they didn't plan on an ambush and kill him.

But tonight, he would stay where he was, with the bed, one end up against the door and across the narrow room.

So, positioning himself on the mattress, on the floor, to the left of the opening door, he laid down. Feeling secure, he even fell asleep.

And then about 2 a.m. he heard something. His eyes popped open. He saw the doorknob turn slowly. Swoop sat up and pulled a pistol from his gun belt on the floor next to him. The door lightly tapped up against the bed frame. Swoop raised the pistol, eye level. He quietly stood. He waited...

Then the door crashed in as far as it would open. The bed moved back about a foot, and a forearm and hand holding a big knife appeared in Swoop's view!

Swoop was inches away now from the hand and shot the back of the hand. The center of the hand suddenly exploded into a black, white and red eruption. The knife fell onto the bed frame. A man outside the door yelled out pitifully and the hand yanked back and out of sight.

Swoop kicked the bed frame aside with two thrusting kicks to clear the door as he sent the chair atop the bed flying. He flung the door open and entered the hall, pistol first. The walkway was empty. He inched down the dark hall and turned into the church. It was dark and empty. The once burned front doors and frame now had long branches hammered across the opening. He dashed to the church, courtyard doors, which were always left open. The courtyard too, was quiet, dark and empty. He looked down and there was no blood trail.

Where did this knifer go? Probably to the staff dorm, but he thought going there a big trap. He just stood there and stared at the vacant courtyard. Nothing. No one even responded to the sound of the solo gunshot, which was somewhat muffled inside his room, yes, but must have broadcast a bit through the silent night.

Frustrated he made his way back to his room. He lit a candle. The dropped knife was rather unique, and its handle, foreign looking. Swedish perhaps, Swoop thought. At any rate he would find out tomorrow. Who will be absent from their duties? Who had his hand virtually blown apart. Whose knife was this? He carried the candle over the wall beside the door.

His bullet went right through the attacker's hand and stuck in the wall. He reset his security measures with the bed frame in place and returned to his mattress on the floor. Now wide awake, he turned the knife over and over, imagining it stuck in him multiple times. Then he blew out the candle and eventually, somehow, fell asleep again.

The next morning, he dressed, complete with guns, his knife on his belt, and with the previously dropped knife in his hand. He walked through the church and Svenson was not there as usual standing guard at the front doors. No one was.

When he entered the mess hall, it was full for breakfast. All the deacons and nuns that were not cooking or serving were seated at the two long tables, along with Father Penance. The Orphans sat eating their gruel on the far side of the hall. Swoop walked up to the staff tables and tossed the knife right into a table. It struck with a vibrating "thwang," that startled everyone. It was a five-foot toss, and even some of the kids across the room saw him do it.

"Somebody lost this in my room last night," Swoop declared.

They all looked at the knife, looked at each other and then back up at Swoop. Swoop walked to the bar and got a cup of coffee. He came back and remained standing, putting a boot up on an empty chair seat.

"Svenson is not guarding the church door this morning. Anybody seen him around?" Swoop said.

No one said anything. Ambrose never stopped eating.

"I will check," Father Penance finally said, standing and wiping his mouth.

"I think I will go with you," Swoop said calmly as he pulled the knife from the table. He set his coffee cup down over the hole.

The two left and crossed the courtyard.

"And how did this knife get in your room? Dropped?" Father Penance asked.

"Somebody tried to stab me to death last night. I shot his hand. That was all I could see as he came in. He dropped the knife."

"Svenson?"

"I don't know. I just saw his arm through the opening of my door. We'll soon see whose left hand will never work anymore," Swoop said.

Inside the staff dorm building they heard some mumbling from a room.

"Here," Father Penance said, and he opened the door without knocking.

Inside, sat a very pale, jaw-dropped, exhausted looking and panting Svenson with his left hand bandaged in dirty white cloth, stained with blood. A half-dressed nun on her knees sat beside him. They both looked at Swoop and the priest.

"Hole in your hand?" Swoop asked.

"Fuck you!" Svenson said.

"No, fuck you and the hole in your hand."

Svenson groaned, showing a lot of teeth. This serious wound had invaded the strength of his whole body.

"You bother me again and I'll put a hole in your head," Swoop said. He looked around the disheveled room. Lots of blood stains.

"What…why…" Father Penance started to ask.

"Oh, he need not explain, Father," interrupted Swoop. "It's all gotten to be very obvious."

Swoop dropped the knife on the dirty floor.

"Here's your new left-handed knife, since you'll never use your right hand again. If I ever see the silver part of it again, I'll kill ya'."

Swoop left and the priest remained. He walked back to the mess hall and stood before the big tables of the staff.

"Sven tried to kill me last night. I will be gone tomorrow," he announced. "Never to return and never to think about any of you sons-a-bitches again. You all would be wise to best...leave...me...be."

He filled a plate of bacon, eggs and bread. With another cup of coffee, he sat at an empty table on the orphan's side of the room and ate, his Thunderer out and atop the table next to him and his hat.

Chapter 21: The Stringer Brothers, the Transporters

Swoop wandered both inside and outside the compound through this possible last day for his Charles Last persona, hopefully his last full day there. Half of this time he sat on the rising hill out back, reading the Jules Verne book and sometimes staring at the horizons. Where in this whole world could he escape to in 80 days? From this high up he could oversee the whole compound and the mesa across the river from where he first spotted the fires of the church. He contemplated the spot beside the river where he collapsed and almost died.

At about 4 p.m. he spied some movement on the river road. Riders approached from the west. When close enough, he identified Deacon Munday and three strangers.

Were these three men with Munday the expectant saviors? The Stringer brothers? Were there two or three brothers? Transporters? Wishing he still had his telescope that the Wells Fargo agents stole first, and then the Indians stole second, the three strangers looked to Swoop like dirty middle-aged, cowboys, not exactly church-orphanage organizers. And no transport wagons? Where were the wagons with which to move all these kids?

The four rode into the stables, and Swoop stood with a grunt, patted the dirt off the butt of his pants and walked down from the rise and into the stables behind them.

"Well, well, this here is Mister Charles Last," Munday said as the men dismounted, "this here is the feller I was telling you about. The man who brought the Indian attack with him and then beat the Indians off."

"Oh?' the oldest stranger said.

"Pastor Wells, Pastor June, Pastor Milon," Munday said.

No hands were shaken. Swoop doubted they were real pastors or in any way that those were their real names. Not only were they filthy, upon close inspection, all were well armed. They were not the Stringer brothers he expected, but two of them surely resembled each other, maybe like brothers?

"These are the men here to pick and transport the orphans tomorrow," Munday said to Swoop.

"You don't have wagons with you?" Swoop asked.

"They ahhh…no. Ahhh, they're coming tomorrow," one man said.

"The Stringer brothers will bring the wagons?" Swoop asked.

This mention seemed to surprise the four of them.

"Ah yes," Munday said, "they will. How'd you know about the Stringer brothers?"

"Penance told me yesterday the Stringer brothers were coming. Said that Stringer brothers would be arriving to pick up the orphans."

"Ohhhh, yeah," Munday said, "Yeah. They show up tomorrow, morning. Yeah. Maybe tonight. Leave tomorrow afternoon."

Since the broken-jawed Williams had never returned, or if he had, he'd remained well hidden away from Swoop in their dorm, another deacon was running the stable. That man gathered the horses' reins.

"I hear tell you walk around here like you're the marshal of the place," this Pastor June said, exposing lots of bad teeth and a deep, southern drawl. He put a hand on his hip, further exposing his holstered pistol.

"I may walk around, but I'm no marshal."

"Ha!" Pastor June barked.

Munday looked a bit nervous and quickly said, "Let's go see what food they have brewing for dinner."

The four walked off, further ignoring Swoop. Not only did they stink, but their story stunk too. He watched as the quartet did not head for the mess hall but rather the deacon and nun dorm. They entered and, in a moment, there were loud celebratory hoots and hollers from inside.

"There you are, you ol' sons of a bitches!"

Swoop overheard Ambrose yell, obviously old friends but not a very pious reunion. Swoop grunted. He shook his head about what to do now. He would for sure be sleeping outside and up on the slope that night. But he also worried about the kids falling into the hands of such obvious low-lives.

At dinnertime, five nuns carried the staff meals across the courtyard from the mess hall and into the dorm building. Swoop watched as the nuns were smiling and giggling as they juggled the plates on trays. They made two trips.

About 10 p.m. Swoop gathered up his blanket and towel for a pillow and cautiously left his room. Ground fires were extinguished in the courtyard, and all was dark but things were oddly noisy from the staff dorm. To stay in the shadows, he walked along the walls and was bound to head out through the stables to the north hill, but such a path put him very near those staff dorm rooms. Inside, bright kerosene lamps lit their main room brightly, so he gave that set of windows a wide berth, but he could still peek inside.

Ambrose, some nuns and the three new transport "pastors," along with a few deacons sat at a big table, smoking cigars and drinking what looked like whiskey. Whiskey bottles were on the table. They were all in some stage of partial undress! What? Half-naked or so, even the nuns, all playing cards.

Ambrose, his head hair wild, was almost completely naked. Laughing and shouting, it was apparent to Swoop that they were all playing…strip poker, and at that very moment a nun lost, cussed and removed her underwear. Swoop had to stop and watch for a few seconds. Deacons? Nuns? Pastors? All drinking whiskey, smoking and playing strip poker? What in hell's bells name was going on in there? All he could think about was leaving sometime tomorrow.

He made it through the stables and walked north a bit into the crisp night air. He threw the blanket down, took off his hat and rolled up the towel for a pillow. He laid down, folded his arms across his chest hoping for sleep, wondering what tomorrow might bring. The kids go west? Now, does he go west too? Does he follow these kids to see where these slimy pastors are taking them? Might make some sense, because bounty hunters pursuing him would assume he'd keep running east and going back west might be a smart, deceptive move? Where in the world, when in the next 80 days, would these kids end up?

Chapter 22: Earliest Bird, the Worm Catcher

A horse's snort. Up on the hill, Swoop awoke at that sound and sat up. He opened up and looked at his pocket watch, moving it to catch some moonlight on the dial. It was just about 3 a.m., and two horsemen left the stables in a slow walk. They headed west on the river road. He watched them disappear. Due to the distance and the dark, he could not see who they were. He laid back down and despite the small mystery, fell back asleep.

Metal rattling. Muffled orders. Whimpering. Swoop awoke again. It was 5 a.m. He leaned up on his elbows and looked below. Three metal wagons, large, metal prisoner transport wagons like the one in the barn were outside, beside the barn doors. They were full of the orphans! Several men afoot circled the wagons.

"Be quiet! You don't want to wake up the deacons and nuns, now," a man ordered in a growling whisper loud enough for Swoop to discern even way up on the rise.

"What the…" Swoop also whispered, but only to himself. "So much for the afternoon departure." He figured they were sneaking the kids out and off.

Three men, probably the three, strip poker "pastors," climbed aboard and started steering the wagons back to the river road, their three horses tied to the backs of the wagons. Each wagon was pulled by a team of two horses. By the time Swoop buttoned and belted up, the two wagons were off and gone. He jogged down the rise and entered the stables. Munday was still there inside.

"They gone? At this hour?" Swoop asked.

"They?"

"The kids!"

"Where did you come from?" Munday said in exasperation.

Swoop did not answer.

"Oh, ah, the kids, yeah, the boys…the pastors wanted an early head start on the day. Early worm, you know." Swoop just stood there, thinking.

"Well, I best be getting back to bed," Munday said. "All the kids are gone. Every last one of them. It'll be quiet around here for a spell."

Swoop made for the twin's horse and started prepping Classy or Sassy.

"Where you going?" Munday asked. "You ain't leaving now too? You should wait till after breakfast to say good-bye. I understand Father Penance is going to give you some traveling money, and a horse, ahhh, yeah, maybe the one you're saddling up right now. A beauty."

"I ain't leaving-leaving," Swoop said. "And weren't the twins supposed to leave with their horses?"

"I don't know nothin' about that. Well, the kids will be fine. They don't need your help anymore."

Swoop just glared at Munday and tightened the saddle. Munday watched him as Swoop left the barn.

Munday made for the dorm and woke up Ambrose and Father Penance. They met in the dorm's big meeting room.

Munday lit a lantern on the table. The two sleepy men sat in chairs. Father Penance was in a sleeping gown and Ambrose still buck naked from his "losses" the night before.

"Charles Last was awake," he told them. "He just walked in on me in the barn after the wagons left."

"From his room?" Ambrose asked.

"No. From the outside. He was fully dressed. Came in from the outside!"

"He was…outside?" Ambrose said.

"Yeah. He saddled up a twin's horse and took off after the wagons."

"What did he say?" Ambrose asked.

"He didn't say much of anything. He asked about the kids. Then he just gave me the stink eye, got a horse and took off. He went west."

"Welllll, hell," Ambrose said as he stood up. "Let me get dressed and you and me will ride off after them. See what's going on. The wagons move slow. We got time to catch up. make some coffee will ya?"

"What's Last up to now?" Father Penance asked.

"He ain't wise to us yet, otherwise he'd a probably killed all of us by now," Ambrose said with a disgusted sigh. "He still thinks the kids are off to a bigger orphanage. Probably we need to catch up to them all, and… and… the kids are locked up in the cages, don't much matter what they see now…probably Stringers will kill him."

"You think?" Munday asked.

"Yeah, Maybe. The Stringers are a tough bunch. They will kill him."

"Won't be easy," the priest said.

"Back shot'll do. And we got our money. Last is their problem now. Well, we do need the Stringer's for the future. Maybe we'll ride out there, catch up to them. See what's happening?"

Munday started coffee in the cafeteria. Ambrose got

dressed. Father Penance nervously rubbed his hands as he went back to his bedroom in the church. Nothing went as expected, as planned, with this Charles Last.

Coffee brewing, Munday got two horses ready in the barn. Dawn would break soon. After a bit, Ambrose strolled into the cafeteria and poured a cup of hot black coffee. Munday was waiting for him, drinking his mug.

They didn't seem to be in much of a hurry. They started walking to the barn, but then, way, way off in the distance, they heard the low rumble of gunshots. They glared at each other for a few seconds.

"That what I…" Munday started.

"Probably," then Ambrose ordered Munday, "Shit. Okay. Best go wake up Clarence too, hell, wake up all the men and women too. Get everybody loaded up and out here now! We're gonna see what alls happening with the Stringers. We'll leave a few behind but most of us will check this out."

"Maybe the Stringers kilt Last?" Munday said. "that what that was."

"Maybe, but we're all going to finish this. I'll start saddling up the horses and we'll be out there shortly." Munday left for the rooms.

Chapter 23: Wagon Loads of Death

A few minutes earlier…

It took about 15 minutes for Swoop to catch up to the three wagons that were moving, single file at a normal but quick pace. Once near them, the three wagons were very tall and long, much bigger than the caged wagon back the barn.

"It's Mister Last," Luke Grisham whispered, and all the orphans watched as Swoop rode up right behind the last wagon. One man drove this wagon and his one horse was tied to the back of the cage.

As Swoop drew near, he put a pointy finger vertical up to his lips at them, signaling for them to remain quiet. He passed the rear wagon with only one driver who looked at him funny and surprised. Swoop smiled big at him, waved and pointed to the first wagon with two fingers as though he was going to speak with those drivers.

The lead wagon had two horses tied to the back for two men. Swoop approached the front wagon's box with the other two men.

"What chu' you doing here?" the passenger side man asked, looking down at him from the great height and the one closest to Swoop. He was "riding shotgun," up in the front box, and he was indeed holding a shotgun. He was not one of the three "pastors" that had arrived the day before. Total stranger. The man with the reins never looked Swoop's way.

"Where are the Stringer brothers?" Swoop asked.

"They can't make it."

"Hey, where are you fellers going? Spokane?" Swoop said with a smile.

"What's it to you?" this front passenger said.

"I might just go with ya." Swoop answered. "I need to go there."

"You from the orphange?"

"Yes sir. I quit. My momma's sick and I gotta' go."

"Well, we ain't a going to no Spokane, Mister. We're headed first to Pendleton's Mining Camp and drop off three or four of these pretty girls and a pretty boy."

"There's an orphanage there?"

"Sheet-nooo', mister," and the man looked like surprised and like he might raise that shotgun, "a brothel!"

It all suddenly became crystal clear to Swoop about the destiny of all these orphans. Swoop drew and shot the man right in the head.

The man fell over on the driver. The shocked driver tried to pull his pistol, but the dead man fell into his way. Swoop drew reins on his horse and the tall wagon continued forward. He dropped back.

The driver got his pistol out, but Swoop went out of the driver's sight. The now brain-dead stranger tumbled forward between the wagon and the horses, and the right front wheel ran right over his torso. The creaks and rattles of the old metal wagon covered over the breaking noise of crushing bones. The teens and kids in the first wagon screamed.

The driver stopped the wagon and he leapt from the seat. The second and third driver behind him, confused, stopped their wagons too. More screams and shouts now followed from the kids in the backs of both wagons.

Swoop dove off his horse and hit the ground hard and rolled. He could see the first driver land on the far side of the first wagon and start for the rear.

The stuttering steps of his horse were in and out of Swoop's way, but from his prone position Swoop fired at the driver's legs visible to him from under the wagon. When given clear shots, he fired three fast shots and two of the rounds splintered the man's legs down to the bone.

"What the…" the driver cried out in a shriek. It was as though his legs were hit by a sledgehammer, and he fell almost face first and now in Swoop's full view. Swoop's horse bucked off from the shots and Swoop managed two more shots hitting the man's chest. The driver grunted, rolled over and laid still. Probably dead.

But the second wagon driver stood in his box, fumbled with a draw and shot as he turned and started climbing down the far side of his tall wagon. The man dropped back as Swoop popped up and dashed to the first wagon's front. He crouched down in front of the two-horse team.

"Get down kids!" Swoop demanded. He could only imagine the third driver dismounted also.

He stepped back from the horses increasing his view of both sides of the first wagon. Without looking down at his guns, he holstered the left gun and reloaded the right one very quickly, his eyes up and peeled on the wagon sides.

With one gun out, Swoop dropped his hat to the ground and scaled up and over the two horse wagon harness, between the two horses and leapt to the front of the wagon seats. He presumed the other two drivers would expect him to appear at the sides of the front wagon, not atop it! He soon was about 20 feet up. He laid on the metal roof and crawled to the rear, to a "peek-point" where he could peer down to the ground.

The second driver was crouched and standing by the right front wheel of the wagon, his head swiveling left and right. Swoop took aim and shot the man in the chest. He bolted back in shock, stepped back and Swoop shot him again.

"Give it up, you madman cunt ,you!" The third driver shouted, still out of sight, "er' I'll start butcherin' these kids!"

The voice came more from the left side of the third wagon. Swoop holstered, rolled to his right and using the crossbars as hand and toe holds, he climbed down.

He peeked over the left side of the second wagon. He saw that 3rd driver standing beside the cage of his wagon. His pistol barrel lay on and in one of the cage's horizonal bars.

Pistol in hand and up, Swoop stepped into view and slowly walked closer. He wanted to try and see where the orphans in the cage were.

"What's up now, hotshot? You'd best just geet' on outta' here with yer' skin intact.

All the kids within the cage naturally took far sides

from the pistol point, but that didn't mean they couldn't be shot with an easy barrel directional shift in a second.

"Drop them pistolas or there will be young blood a drippin' off this craft!" the man hollered.

"You know, there's no way you come out of this alive," Swoop said calmly. "You start shooting kids and I'll turn you into a honeycomb."

"You think!"

"I know," Swoop said, now smiling.

That smile! The nervous man spent too much time looking at Swoop. His gun barrel deep and still resting on a cross bar of the cage, but it now nervously twitched in deep and then out shallow. Luke Gresham was in that third wagon and Swoop saw him step forward, eyes bearing down on that shifting deep and shallow gun barrel.

Luke lunged out and grabbed the few inches of barrel when it stuck well inside the cage. The man felt the grip, looked at Luke, and Luke's face was the last thing the man saw, as Swoop blew his head and neck to bits with four .41 caliber rounds. The bullet-butchered kidnapper dropped.

"He's got the key in his vest pocket," Luke cried out.

"Is there another man!" Swoop yelled out.

"One of them rode ahead," Luke said.

"How long ago?" Swoop asked.

"When we started out back at the church."

"Gallop? Trot? Or Walk?"

"Trot," Luke said.

Swoop holstered and searched the dead man's pocket, extracting a key. He stepped to the back gate of the wagon and unlocked the padlock. Luke jumped out and the others wanted to follow.

"No! Hold on, kids. We've got to get out of here. And fast," Swoop shouted loud enough to all the orphans in both wagons. "The deacons at the church will no doubt be racing here right now."

The kids stopped and backed up.

"Luke, get the key for the front wagon padlock. The kids up there should know who has it."

"That one does!" Foley Delane, paying attention to the voices, shouted from the first wagon's cage and pointing down to the crushed man below them.

Luke ran to the first man Swoop shot and hauled him out from under the wagon. His chest was indeed ruined, a few broken ribs even pierced his shirt and jacket, the bones visible. He searched his pockets for the key. He found it, unbent in a side pants pocket. He undid the corpse's gun belt buckle and yanked it free. He strapped on the gun belt. Then he dashed around the wagon to the second man and stripped him of his belt, He found the driver's pistol, shoved it in the holster and threw the gun belt over his shoulder.

Swoop watched him work. Luke looked to him like many a too-young, sharp, smart soldier that had served under his command through the decades, and probably much like his own 15-year-old self when he lied about his age and joined the Army too young.

Swoop took the gun belt off the man by the second wagon driver he'd just shot, collected the loose pistol and holstered the weapon. He tied the reins of his horse to the back of the cage of the second wagon, beside the other horse.

Luke unlocked the chain of the first wagon's cage.

"Now listen kids," Swoop yelled, "you all hold the door chains tight, so the doors don't swing open, and so no one falls out. Luke, can you drive this second wagon?"

"I can. Certainly," Luke said, as he picked up the dropped shotgun.

"Who can handle the third wagon?"

"I can," a teenage girl said.

"Do so. I don't know how far we can get. But I'll be making a plan," Swoop said. "We've got to go. Now!"

"There's a rifle up here," Luke said, while boarding the second wagon.

"Good. You've got that scatter gun. Toss me the rifle," Swoop said as he walked up to him.

He snatched the rifle in the air and looked up at him, eye to eye. "Stay close kids and follow me."

"To hell and back, sir," Luke said.

"Can you, will you shoot some of these sons a bitches if they catch up to us?"

"I can, I will."

Swoop winked at him but thought they all might end up in hell and not coming back from it. He ran to the front of the first wagon.

"Who in here can steer this rig if I need them too?" Swoop shouted into the cage.

Several volunteered.

"Good," and Swoop pointed to the oldest teenage boy who raised his hand to join him. "Okay, I may have to jump off and hold those deacons off at some point. You might have to carry on."

"They'll kill ya, Mister Last!" Foley Delane shouted out, his voice cracking.

"Maybe so," Swoop said.

The two got up into the driver's box and Swoop ran those reins hard enough on the horses to get them moving to a trot.

"What's yer name, kid?"

"Laramie Tops, sir," the teen said.

Swoop nodded and pointed to the gun belt on the box floor.

"Strap that 'one-eyed-scribe' on Laramie."

The kid buckled the gun belt on. Swoop knew it would take a major miracle to get out of this one alive.

Chapter 24: Wells Fargo, the Agents Arrive
Dawn broke...

The three wagons turned a sharp corner around a jagged rocky rise and there were three horsemen walking in the middle of the river road. All surprised to see each other. The wagons and the three horses stopped.

"Ge...General? General Mordecai Swoop Swellen?" shouted an astonished Colonel Calico Reems.

"Colonel Anthony Calico Reems?" answered Swoop, just as amazed. He looked at the two men with his old Army friend.

"Canary?" Swoop added. "and Rory Pickles?"

"That's us General," Canary said.

"What...what in the tar-est of nations are you doing with three prisoner wagons full of...of kids, Swoop?" Calico Reems said.

Swoop jumped off the wagon and ran up to the men.

Luke jumped off the second wagon and ran up to them too, shotgun in hand, and when he got next to Swoop, Swoop had to push the gun barrel down and away from the three horsemen.

"Calico, I am rescuing these kids. They are not my prisoners. They are all orphans held in a fake church, a fake orphanage. These kids were sold into prostitution in mining camps and cities west of here. Who knows exactly where. Boys, girls, teenagers raped and molested. I know that you and I have no doubt, unsightly business. I can guess why you are here, but not for now. We have these kids' lives to save. The gang chasing us, is coming up behind me."

"How many?"

"Maybe Ten?" Swoop said. "Maybe more and they will be upon us soon. Calico…I can't stop em' alone. The fact you showed up here? Now? Is kind of a miracle. A major miracle."

"This all true, son," Calico Reems leaned to the right and had to ask Luke.

"It's all true, sir. We are in big trouble. We have no time!"

"I…I believe you Swoop. How far behind are they?"

"I figure about ten minutes?"

"All of em' scoundrels?" Calico asked.

"Every last one of em, Colonel. Did you pass a solo rider on the road?"

"We did."

"Well, he was one of them. He went on ahead to set up the sales of these kids."

"Sales! Looks like this turn is tight right here and is a goodly corner for a surprise," Calico Reems said looking around. "We did not see ner' hear those metal wagons until we turned upon you. I think this is a goodly place to stop em.' Roundin' this hard corner."

Swoop smiled and said, "I don't think they will expect me to stop and emboscada em.' But with you three, now we can. Luke, get those wagons over there, off the road, and over in the corner. Get all orphans out of the wagons and up in those rocks. If we four lose the fight? Tell them to scatter. Tell them go west. Which is…that way." He pointed. "And give me that shotgun."

"I…I can fight em too, sir," Luke said, "I can. make that five, sir."

"Well then, alright. Here's the rifle. You will be the last resort if they get through us. Take cover around the wagons and shoot. Cover, you hear me! Stay down low and behind cover, peeking out with one eye and gun. Don't stand up and shoot. Stay low. And know where we are hiding. Don't shoot us."

"Yes, sir."

Calico Reems studied Luke and Swoop guide the group unloading from the wagons, and then finally he examined the terrain of this pending battle. Canary tied off the agent's horses a safe distance away. Pickles took a post at the corner staring east on the river road. Swoop joined Reems, Pickles and Canary after a few minutes at that corner.

"What you think?" Swoop asked.

"Well sir, we gotta get em to stop, or they'll turn this corner and run fast right by us. We'll thin them out, but the survivors will regroup over yonder somewhere and come right back upon us. On or off the road. Probably off. Maybe on foot, through those rocks," Canary said.

"We may miss half of em. We gotta end this right chere," Pickles said.

"Good assessments," Swoop said. "If we pull the wagons more forward, still to the side, but right over there, they'll round the bend and see it when they all make the turn. They'll probably see the wagons, stop and wonder, 'what the hell the wagons are do-in' there?'"

"Yeah. Yeah. Then we get em'."

"Then we shoot em', Calico. These are sons a bitches

every last one," Swoop said.

"Reckon so. Reckon," the Colonel said, "they'll start shooting' at us right way anyway. Works out. Works out. The Lord don't need no more squaring away than that, General. Spread us out two and two, Two high. Too low. No crossfire," Reems said.

Swoop nodded.

Swoop and Pickles led the horses to position a wagon to be better seen once a turn was made. Pickles remained at the corner turn and peered east on the river road. There was indeed a cloud of dust in the distance.

"I see em! Theys coming!"

Reems, Canary and Pickles had rifles. Reems positioned his two men out of sight and high to the left. Then he ran over to Swoop. The two slid about 5 feet down the slope on the opposite side and laid flat.

"Think they'll make a cautious turn?" Reems asked.

"Not likely. They all strike me as pretty dumb. As I said, I don't think they'll expect me to stop and ambush them alone."

"Dumb is good," Reems said.

"That it is. Always is." Swoop said.

They waited.

"These kids have been through some Hell," Swoop said.

"Swoop did you kill five of our Wells Fargo agents?" Reems asked.

"No, sir. Actually, the five caught me. Shot my horse out from under me. I went flying, got knocked out when I landed. And when I awoke, I was tied up by them in their camp. I think they were about to kill me. Dead or alive. I was arguing with them about it when some renegade Indians, a split from the local Utes raided the camp. They just knocked me out and took my clothes, but they killed all five of them. Looks to me, they tortured one."

Their eyes remained peeled on the road as Swoop continued, "I think when they found me tied up as a prisoner, they took pity on me or something and let me live. But not too much pity. They left me out in the high desert, canyon area south of here. To die anyway. Slowly. I made it on foot, near dead, to this so-called church. These same Indians then attacked the church. Their chief Nerto had the five badges in his medicine bag when I killed him. The badges are back at the church."

"Where are the bodies, Swoop?"

"About…about 15 miles southwest of the church. Honestly Cal I don't know if you'll ever find em.' Been over two weeks. Animals were already after them. They'll be spread out even more. One of the agents was nicknamed Sugar Bowl."

"I'll be, I've met Sugar. What about the Army bounty hunter, the mountain man Gee Willikers? Did you kill him back in Colorado?"

"No. A woman shot him, and he shot the woman. He wanted the full bounty on me, so he shot her first to keep it all. But she shot him back. I saw it all."

"If the Army knows that, they ain't telling anyone."

"I don't doubt it. I hear from friends that the Army wants me dead so I cannot tell the story, the truth about the Wounded Knee Massacre. How I resisted."

"We knew you were in trouble for desertion," Reems said, "that's all we heard, but none of us could justify the dead or alive charge and such a high bounty. That sounds like the Army."

"This church here is not a church. And the orphanage is not an orphanage. It was this sex gang bartering for kids. There is one real priest there. A sorry one at best. He knows all about it. But the gang must hold something over him."

"Bad past maybe?"

"Maybe. Something like that. But he's the front man for their operation. A guy named Ambrose is the real skunk. The gang leader. I hope I see him turn this corner.”

“Let’s hope he’s one of them a coming,” Reems said as he looked at Swoop and smiled.

Swoop smiled back, but they both knew that if they survived this, they too would have some kind of “bounty-arrest showdown.”

“We’ve done something like this before,” Swoop half-whispered and returned his watch on the road.

“Yessir. Point Ernest, Missouri. Down in the Breaks.”

“The damn Breaks,” Swoop said with a sigh.

“You saved my life. Couple of times I think.”

“And you saved mine,” Swoop said.

“I lost track of the last time to figure who owes who in the end?” Reems said.

Swoop just shook his head at that, and then he said, “Hope we don’t shoot any horses.”

“Yup.”

And then they came. There were 10 of them. In a poor formation on the road, almost bumping into each other.

“Looks like there’s three nuns with em,” Reems whispered.

“They ain’t nuns,” Swoop said, pulling both his Colt Thunderers.

“Dear Lord, please may our aim be true,” Reems started a prayer, “may we slay the evil upon us and may we, the noblest in your service, survive. May we…”

As the gang fully rounded the corner they crashed into each other as Ambrose and a few in the front stopped short. They all looked at an empty wagon just around the bend. Then saw the second wagon tucked further away.

“What the Hell...” one said, pointing at the wagon, “did one break down...”

Those were his last words.

Swoop began firing his two guns, one at a time, hitting the riders. Canary and Pickles opened up with their lever actions.

"...save the blessed chillren' from..." Reems yelled as he shot and shot.

"...the clutches of these evil..."

They worked their lever actions cutting the men and women right off their horses.

"...forces and bring peace into young lives. AMEN!"

"Amen," Swoop added.

Even with a nasty hole through his wounded hand, Svenson was present among them, brought down by rifle fire. Williams was there too, with a big white cloth wrapped like a bonnet full around his head, holding his jaw in place. A rifle round took him off the saddle.

The two fake nuns tried to shoot back at them, and they were blasted, flung off the saddles by rifle and pistol fire, with their handguns flying in twirls through the air.

"Nuns with guns," Reems said.

"They ain't nuns," Swoop said again. Rosy and Bloodworth were not there.

Swoop reloaded as he was a bullet counter and a head counter, and he knew what to do next, feeling that magic moment arrive when veteran cavalry officers knew when to charge, when the momentum was theirs to take. The moment. With two guns blazing, he rose and ran, cutting through the remaining gang. He saw a confused jaw-broken Williams in that bewildered, ambush state, down and wounded on his back, pistol out and not knowing what direction to shoot, up, down, right or left. Swoop blew the top of his head off.

The rifle fire subsided. All that was left was the groaning of the dying and the blasts ringing in the ears. The other three ex-Army men emerged and looked at each other and joined Swoop. The four knew what to do, remove the weapons from all, dead or alive.

"You won't need this where you're going," Canary said

to one, picking up his pistol.

"Where…where my goin' now?" Ambrose said in gasps. "Doctors?"

"Doctors! Sheet bubba," Canary said, "not even a cemetery. You picked a helleva location to die at. And die exposed for all your worth, you shall. You will become a fine dinner fer everything that crawls and flies."

Luke stepped out from a cropping and declared, "I shot me one Mister Last!"

"I don't know if that's good or bad, Luke. But thanks for the help."

None of the horses were hit. They just wandered around. Then all the orphans popped up from their hidey-holes above. They began climbing back down the hillside. As each one got to the flat land, they ran straight up to Swoop. They were all smiling. They hugged him. As each teen and child got near, they tried to hug him and wound up just hugging each other. It became a big pile of kids and a big man standing in the center, not knowing what to do but snort, rub his nose and wipe the corners of his eyes.

Calico Reems, Canary and Pickles got together, rather amazed at the sight and could only stare at this pile of humanity.

"Well, I'll be damned," Canary said. Will ya' just look at that."

"Yup," Calico Reems said, "Swoop Swellen's orphans."

Chapter 25: Interrupting a Miracle

After a search of the bodies, Swoop and Calico Reems stood beside each other.

"What's next, General?"

"Are you still a U.S. Marshal, Cal?" Swoop asked.

"Through and through."

"This is not over until we clean out the rat's nest back at the church," Swoop said. "Especially Father Penance. A real priest I'd say and the cover for the whole operation. And there's still a straggler or two back there unaccounted for here. If we ignore them? They might regroup and play all this out again and again."

"Yup."

"What say you and me, ride back there," Swoop said. "Let Canary and Pickles take these wagons west with the kids. Then what's closest, for the next day?"

"Spokane. Two days."

"Ooooh. Two days. These kids will go hungry," Swoop said. "I hate to do it, I hate it, but we probably need to get them all back to the church. Feed em' all. Prep em' all for the two-day ride to Spokane."

"We can take them to a real church in Spokane," Reems said. "I know many a place."

"But let's us, you and me, ride ahead and take care of any dirty business before they get there," Swoop said.

"Wise assessment," Reems said.

Swoop gathered all the orphans up.

"We can't go west yet, kids," Swoop started. "Spokane is two days away. You need to eat."

"We ain't had no breakfast, Mister Last," one kid shouted out. "They just kicked us out of bed and run us into these wagons."

"We just have to go back to the church and feed you all. Get rested and these three men will take you to a real church orphanage in Spokane. These are Army men and now Wells Fargo men and this man…this man here is also United States Marshal, Calico Reems. That there is Canary, that's a nickname - Quinton Dew, and that's Rory Pickles."

"Is Pickles a nickname too?" a towheaded little girl asked.

"No ma'am," Rory said, "Pickles is my real name."

"That's a funny name!" she said.

"I know these men for years," Swoop continued, "From the Army. Yes, I was once in the Army. I reckon you will still have to ride in these prisoner wagons again. I'm sorry. But unlocked! That's all we've got, but you are NOT prisoners anymore, you understand. You will be orphaned out proper."

"Will you come with us, Mister Last? To Spokane?" one asked.

"I am afraid not. I…I have some unfinished business to attend to."

"He's been calling you a general," Foley Delane said.

"Well, yes Foley. I was one. Once, yes," Swoop said.

"Figures," another said. Several nodded their heads.

Now the marshal and I are going to ride ahead back to the church first and…and make it all safe. Luke, I'm gonna be taking Sassy again."

"You're riding Classy, not Sassy," Janet Grisham said. "You go on ahead General."

"Classy. I was wondering about that, Janet."

Luke found and was busy struggling with Ambrose's near dead body. Nearly dead, Ambrose was left only to gasp and howl at the movements.

"I'm gonna get…geeet…my…uncle's…gun belt back, General Last," Luke explained. "I found the gun over there."

"You do that, kid," Swoop said.

"What should we do with these scum buckets here? A couple are still alive." Pickles asked Reems and Swoop.

Reems and Swoop exchanged glances.

"I figure they'll be dead soon by the looks of them," Swoop said.

"Leave em' for the devil," Calico Reems said.

"So be it, Sirs," Canary said.

Luke walked up to them, and Swoop almost chuckled. The teen wore a gun belt, had his uncle's gun belt over his shoulder and held a shotgun in his hand. You look like one of us, Luke. You help Canary and Pickles get these kids back to the church," Swoop said.

"Yes, sir."

Swoop and Calico Reems mounted their horses and took off for the church.

"Should we expect trouble?" Calico asked.

"Not at first, but once inside, and they see me again? Alive? Maybe."

"How many left?'

"Three? Four? And the priest."

Neither discussed what Calico, Canary and Pickles would do with Swoop when this was all put to rest. A topic both just hated to discuss. Was their personal bloodshed next? As they rode on, Calico saw 3 bodies lined up, dead on the roadside.

"You do that?" he asked.

"I did. Two of them were the Stringer brothers. The other one was a cohort."

"How'd you shoot all three of em?"

"One at a time. Very tricky too."

Reems chuckled.

"Lucky, I guess," Swoop said. "That kid named Luke helped. He needs to join the Army Cal, but he needs to help his twin sister too."

"Maybe he needs to be a Wells Fargo sidekick," Reems said. "He was sure calm in a storm. He might accompany me and the boys and help us out. His sister could head-quarter with my sister-in-law in St. Louis. And he might officially stay there with her too."

"That sounds like a great idea. She's been raped by these skunks."

"Oh, oh Lord Almighty, those skunk-devils," Reems said.

When the church compound was in sight, Swoop studied the wall tops to see if he could spot any heads watching their approach. None were seen. Swoop pointed to the burned, open stable doors.

"There," he said.

"This place been attacked?" Reems asked.

"Yeah. The Indians that left me for dead after your agents caught me, those Indians that tracked me here, came here en masse to finish me off, and rob the place and kidnap all the females. They saw my wanted poster in one of the agents gear when they killed them and stole their bags. Folks will do a lot for $1,000, Indian or no Indian."

Reems' eyebrows raised and he shook his head. He looked around.

"Saints be praised. Like an attack on a fort by the looks of this place."

Swoop just grunted and said, "It was."

They entered through the stables and out into the courtyard. A few nuns and two men walked around doing their chores.

"More fake nuns? Deacons?" Reems asked.

"More fake nuns and deacons," Swoop repeated.

Sister Rosalinda saw him and ran up to his horse.

"What are you doing? They said you left. Did the kids get going all right? Did you come back for me?"

"In a way Rosey, I came back for you. The kids did not get going alright. Rose, this is Marshal Calico Reems, and his men will be here shortly, with all the kids."

"What? The… you mean coming back here?"

"Yeah, I suggest you and whoever is left? Get the Hell out of here."

"I will leave with you!" she said, putting her hand on his saddle horn.

"Rose, I will soon either be arrested or killed off. I suggest you few left vamoose. Or you and everyone here will suffer the same fate."

She took off.

"Whose she?" Reems said.

"A nightmare wrapped in a fever," Swoop said, as he pointed to the doors of the church. "The stragglers left here are half-wit, half-bakes. They won't regroup."

"I still need an insider witness," Reems said. "But we'll see if there's anyone left to testify against. But I'll need a statement about what is going on around here."
Swoop nodded. They dropped reins.

"Hold up Rose!" Swoop shouted, "come on over here."

"Ahhh…Change yer' mind?" She stopped, smiled coyly and said.

"You are under arrest," Reems said and slipped off his horse, and also slipped a pair of hand cuffs from his belt.

"Wha…" Rose started.

"Rosey, you are now a federal suspect or a witness, to a sex gang crime," Swoop advised, shifting in his saddle, "up to you."

Reems handcuffed her and reached back to pull another pair of cuffs draped over his belt. He looked around and he walked her over to one of the water pumps. He used the second pair to cuff her to the main pipe of the pump. Swoop followed them, still on Classy.

"I'll be back," Reems said to her.

"Rose, if you don't witness to what went on here, you'll be in a dark dungeon the rest of your life."

"But I…we…"

"Who knows," Swoop said over his shoulder, "maybe you'll get real religion in prison? Where's Penance?"

"Hell, if I know," a dour Rosey said, "Back in his office probably. Ain't see him."

Swoop pointed to the church doors. They walked their horses to the doors and then into the church, with Reems tailing Swoop. Reems stopped, faced the alter, and made the sign of the cross, then they were off to the far hall and down to Father Penance's office. The door was open, and they walked right in.

Father Penance was seated, calmly at his desk, both hands out of sight.

Reems pulled his pistol.

"Hands on the table, fake Father," he said.

Penance half-smiled and slowly lifted his hands, to reveal rosary beads in one hand.

"I am not a 'fake' Father," Penance said.

"You sound like a fake to me."

"Penance, this here is United States Marshal Calico Reems," Swoop said.

"Oh," Penance said softly. "After your ruckus this morning I half-way expected something like this but not this soon. I did expect that maybe the Stringers would stop you, maybe kill you out on the turnpike though."

"I got lucky. They got all the way unlucky."

"Penance, you're under arrest for kidnapping and for selling kids into prostitution, turning them into sex slaves," Reems said.

Penance fingered the beads on his rosery. He sighed so deeply he coughed and brought up some sputum. He spit into a spittoon beside his desk.

"I was sent here by the church, years ago," the priest said, "because they had to hide me away. I had some, some human, natural desires I just could not control. There was this little Mexican girl…"

"I don't want to hear it," Reems said, "and it don't sound natural to me at all."

"Hmmm, yes. Yes. Well, somehow this gang heard stories about me from rumors at another church. Yes. They saw me as a…a dupe. An easy mark. A figurehead to con people with this orphanage plan. Ambrose…is he…dead?"

"Slow dead," Swoop said.

"Well, good. Ambrose knew what all the drunken and ignorant souls wandering the lands wanted…wanted all kinds of pleasures, man, woman and child. He and his gang were in the prostitute business. Running booze and hookers. All sexes. All ages.   He never could get them young enough. He dreamed up this scheme. He somehow heard about me down south and they all came up here to find me. He threw me up against that wall right there and he took over. They left me alive as a legitimate connection to the church. Or… he would ruin me here too if I didn't comply. But probably

I know, he would just kill me if I didn't listen to him. I guess I will go to prison now? I imagine?"

"Prison," Reems said, lowering his gun.

"Yes," Penance said with a gulp. He turned pale. He laid the rosary beads on the desk. "I presume prison is not a good place for…for what I have done to children?"

"Prison is never a good place," Reems said, "and it won't be any good at all for what you have done. My understanding."

Silence. A pallor fell over Penance.

"Padre," Swoop said, "where's your gun?"

"Hanging behind the door over there."

Swoop got the pistol from the hanging holster, hung the belt with bullets attached in loops around his shoulder and he unloaded the gun but for one bullet, keeping it next in revolver rotation. He laid it on the desk next to the beads. Reems watched all this and was a bit surprised, but he got the message.

Penances' eyes stared at Swoop, and vice versa.

"There ain't no places in Heaven for suicide," Reems warned.

"I have made no reservation for Heaven," Penance said. Reems nodded.

"When you came here, when you showed up," Penance said to Swoop, "you were a blessing and a curse. I sensed a certain finality when we carried you into the church that day. A savior. An executioner. A finality. I saved your life…"

"And I thank you."

"…because I sensed some sort of ending about you. There is some finality about you, Mister Charles Last. A last chance. Is your last name really 'Last.'"

"No, it is not."

"I didn't think so. You are somebody else. A force of nature."

With that, Swoop nodded and left the room, then Reems backed out. Reems closed the door. They walked down the hallway and into the church. By the time they reached the courtyard doors, they heard the single gunshot back down the hall.

They looked at each other. Reems turned to walk back. Swoop extended his arm and leaned against the door frame, his turn to release a deep breath. He watched the remaining two fake nuns and two fake deacons hustle about, packing to leave. He truly wished he could kill them all, but he was very, very tired this mid-morning. The fake sister sat on the rounded brick edge of her attached water pump, dejected and looked back at him with a helpless expression.

After a minute, he heard some mumbling behind him. He turned to see Reems had stopped and kneeled at the worn, wooden alter, praying. Swoop then fully leaned his torso onto the door frame. When finished, Reems stood and walked up to him.

"Yup," was all he said.

Swoop nodded. Father Penance was no more.

"Hey! Hey lady!" Swoop shouted to Sister Bloodworth, "come over here."

She stopped and made a mean face.

"Yeah, come here."

She started toward him. He remembered seeing her that first day he was there, thinking she was a nun of mercy. Now he saw her as the ruthless monster she was.

Swoop snapped his fingers…"The bracelets…"

"You just come and get em.'"

"Lady...if I have to come over there to you and get em,' I'll chop your fucking hands off to do it."

She sneered, narrowed out her hands and slid the Gresham bracelets off. She dropped them on the dirt.

"If you like all the teeth still in your mouth, you'll pick those up and hand them to me."

She bent over, grabbed them and walked up to Swoop. She gave the bracelets to him, turned and left.

Reems shook his head. Swoop spun the bracelets on a finger.

"Stolen?" Reems asked.

"Stolen."

The first of three prisoner wagons full of the smiling, noisy kids appeared through the stables and into the courtyard and with 7 horses tied to the back. Reems caught Swoop half-smiling.

Hours later…

As per Swoop's suggestion, the orphans invaded the now empty staff dormitory rooms. If any of them came with belongings such as the Gresham twins, all their property was ransacked and kept in there. Clothes, musical instruments, heirlooms, jewelry, books, sometimes even some furniture. If the staff hadn't used it or stolen it, it was kept in a big room. For some of the orphans captured there for weeks, it was like a birthday or Christmas.

Then they ate. They were fed by whatever food that Swoop, Reems, Canary and Pickles could rustle up in the kitchen. Rosey was forced into kitchen duty. There was a relieved atmosphere of a party in the mess hall. A teenage girl sang and played her recovered guitar. It reminded Swoop of the old summer, family barbeques back at Fort Shannon, which was the last time, years ago to his count, he actually felt a few moments of true calm, happiness.

Whatever they concocted to eat was a damn-sight better than the half-gruel the kids usually ate.

"I think that I will take the Gresham twins back with me to St Louis," Reems told Swoop. "I like the idea of that Luke kid side-kicking with us at Wells Fargo. With me. Like I said, the girl can stay with my sister and her family there. The boy too when we are back home."

"That would be terrific," Swoop said, wolfing down some scrambled eggs.

There was still no conversation about Swoop's fate. No handcuffs. No announcements. Swoop contemplated an escape. After the meal, he stood and wandered outside without an objection. He was in the courtyard alone. He then re-entered the church as far deep as to walk into Penance's office.

The single gunshot to the head had tossed the priest's body way out of the chair and left him sprawled out on the floor, the pistol dropped by the desk. The flies had magically weaved their way in, buzzing and busy. Swoop walked around the desk and started pulling open the drawers. In the third drawer he found Nerto's medicine bag. He felt of it, and the badges were still inside. He took it. Behind the bag was a roll of paper money. He counted it. One hundred and twenty-one dollars. It was blood money, for sure, but he needed any he could find. He took that too.

"General, can we talk outside?"

Surprised, Swoop looked up to see Calico Reems standing in the doorway. The Marshal saw him retrieve the bag and money. Swoop lifted and shook the medicine bag for him to see. Reems turned and left. Swoop had little choice but to follow.

Outside, he was also greeted by Pickles and Canary. The four stood in a group, Swoop tense. Weapons all holstered.

"Here is Nerto's medicine bag, Calico. Inside are the 5 badges of your 5 dead agents the Indians killed," Swoop said and handed Reems the leather sack.

Reems looked a little astonished and took the bag. He pulled the drawstring rim apart and looked inside. They were touchstones of the death of friends and co-workers. Then he shoved the bag in his jacket pocket.

"General, we know you left Fort Shannon just before

the Massacre at Wounded Knee. Those other soldiers there, if they were half the man you were, they'd a left too. With ya," Reems said.

"I guess that's debatable Colonel," Swoop said to all the three agents.

"There has been considerable bad publicity about the massacre coast-to-coast," Reems said. "It's like Wounded Knee is the last Indian massacre the general public could stand. A tide has started to turn in this country about killing Indians like that."

Swoop nodded.

"Canary and Pickles and me…we'd been talking," Reems said. "We figure that you are a dead man with that wanted dead or alive bounty. If they keep you alive and try to court martial you, if you have a public trial, the horrible story of Wounded Knee, it would be all out again and in the news. Liven' it all over again. The public would turn in your favor, and agin' the Army. The public would probably regard you as some kind of smart hero. The Army can't have that."

"I don't know, maybe," Swoop said.

"Considering the Knee…and considering you didn't kill Gee Willikers down in Colorado, and you didn't kill our 5 detectives out on the desert, and all this here that you have done to save these kids and all. You coming here Swoop…is a kind of miracle."

Canary and Pickles shuffled their feet and smiled at Swoop.

"And I just can't abide by interrupting a miracle," Reems said. "We think it's a shame that such a noble man as yourself has to live in such an exile. We are just going to officially report that you…you did all this good here that you did, and you…escaped. Just flat out slipped right through our greasy fingers."

"Having such nobility among us is worth more than $1,000," Canary said, "especially, you know, split three ways!" He ended that with a laugh.

"Four ways!" Pickles added. "Wells Fargo has to get a cut of the bounty too. It's the rules."

Swoop rubbed a palm over his mouth and just stood there.

"So, I guess you'd best escape then!" Reems said. "But first, fill up your bags with grub and matches, and then just…just escape on us… whew… like a…like a ghost." He waved his hand in the air. "We've got to go back west with these kids. Then we've got coastal pirates to catch."

"I thank you gentlemen," Swoop said and nodded. Relieved he would not have to battle with these old friends, he walked across the yard to the Gresham twins.

"Janet. Luke. The Marshal says he wants to take you two back to St. Louis. To stay at his sister's. And Luke he may have a job in mind for you with the company."

"Well…I…we…" Luke started.

"That sounds just fine, General," Janet said.

"I ahhh, I'm not a general anymore," Swoop added. "And listen, can I have Classy? I really need to leave. And there are plenty of horses here now you all can have. Classy and I have become…"

"I should think so," Janet said.

Luke nodded.

"I will treat him like a lost son."

"We love him, sir. So, you do treat him, treat him thusly. As we know you would treat…an orphan."

Swoop got the message, and he felt a swelling in his chest. He sort of stammered a few sounds that wheezed out in little gasps as he lowered his head so that his hat brim would cover most of his face.

"Goodbye…kids," he said, still hiding his face. "Don't ahhh, don't tell anybody I'm leaving, okay? I don't want to create a ruckus."

They nodded their heads.

He went to his room and gathered up what little he had there. The Jules Verne book. A smattering of clothes. He looked at the two arrows standing up in the corner, the ones he'd scavenged from the canyon's desert. As he did before on his trek, he stuck one in each pocket, arrowhead buried.

Then it was his turn to scour the staff dorm. He looked around and turned things over. He took a bottle of whiskey, a telescope, a gun cleaning kit and he found several small cardboard boxes of ammo for his Colts and for the dead, Randy's rifle – the one Ambrose never got to "collect" from him.

Pocket's full, he left and walked across the yard and into the kitchen, where he filled up some canvas bags of canned goods.

Then next to the stables. He saddled up Classy and tossed the bags over the horse and was about to mount the steed. He wanted to walk the horse out through the courtyard and church but he would be seen leaving. He didn't want the rest of the orphans to see him leave, but the Wells Fargo men did follow him to the barn.

"General," Reems said shaking his hand.

"General," Canary said, shaking his hand next.

"General," Pickles said, last to shake his hand.

"May the good Lord bless and keep you," Reems said.

"Now go ahead now. Escape will ya,' before somebody makes us change our minds. We'll take good care of these youngins.' Ima' gonna put the twins on trains to St. Louis when we get back."

Swoop and Classy quietly walked through the barn doors and out on the river road where he mounted up out front. He took another good look at where he'd collapsed across the river. And then he trotted off eastward. Glad and sad.

After about an hour, he stopped Classy, pulled the arrow heads from his pockets, now uncomfortably somewhat horizontal in those pockets, and he tossed them down beside the road. He thought that maybe some children, or some collectors might find those arrowheads alone someday, a hundred years or more from now and consider these damn murderous things as some sort of treasure with a mysterious past. If they only knew…

Chapter 26: Sagiswatch, the No Waking Nightmare
Day's later, well after midnight…

The man crept up and stood over the sleeping form that had a hat and a head on the grounded saddle, the body under a blanket. It was a cold camp. Dark. The man smiled and raised a machete high in the air over the sleeper that he'd been following for days.

"Hey! Hobo general," he whispered, "What? Mister General! You have no nightmare this time to warn you of danger? HA!"

"Heeey, Sagiswatch," a voice said quietly from behind him. Swoop Swellen emerged from a collection of rocks off to the right, a pistol in his hand.

A very surprised Sagiswatch spun to see him. Then he looked back down at the stuffed form on the ground below him, then back up at Swoop. He kicked the form to see a pile of blankets and box. A towel made for a head in the hat.

"You have to be asleep to have a nightmare," Swoop said. "I am wide awake, watching you from over here."

Sagiswatch was still shocked and speechless.

"As for you? Your nightmare? Right now, your nightmare is when you are wide awake," Swoop said and shot him twice in the chest.

Sagiswatch dropped the machete, gasped and clutched his chest, stumbling back. Swoop matched his step, walked forward as the Indian stutter-stepped backward. From the hip, he shot him again. Both Swoop's horse and Sagiswatch's horse, hidden nearby, whinnied and snorted with each surprise round fired. Hooves moved small rocks.

Sagiswatch fell on his back, coughing. His tremoring right hand tried to touch his pistol in his holster. Swoop shot the forearm, incapacitating the attempt. He reached over and took the pistol.

"I've seen you behind me for two days now. Yeah. You'll die right out here. Yeah. There won't be no burning canoe on a lake for you. No burning cabin. No raising smoke and ash. You'll just rot away out here like a coyote turd being picked apart by vultures."

"I…will come back…and haunt you."

"Don't think so. You only haunted me when you were alive. And I just fixed that," Swoop said.

"You…" he started.

"I?" Swoop said.

And Sagiswatch died.

Swoop peeled Sagiswatch's gun belt off and put the pistol back in it. He tossed the rig by his bedroll. He scanned the landscape where he thought he'd heard Sagiswatch's noisy horse. He wandered over and found him by a tree and some grass. It was the same horse that charged and knocked him airborne weeks earlier back in the canyon's desert. There were saddlebags of various supplies and food still tied to the saddle. He rummaged through one and found the same kind of jerky he once ate, which he stuck in his pocket.

"You're okay wild man," he told the horse, patting its neck. "Let's go. Come on. Meet a friend."

He and the horse walked back to the cold camp and near Classy.

"Classy, this is….ahhh…Sagis," he invented the name, "Sagis, Classy. You two will become good friends. We're going to Canada. I'll bet neither of you have been to Canada. Neither have I."

He took the bags, saddle and blanket off the newly re-named horse and laid them down by a short tree. Then he walked back to Sagiswatch. The Indian had a pretty decent wool jacket and Swoop stripped the corpse of it. Only two bullet holes, one in the sleeve, one through the chest. Since the man wore the jacket open, it was spared the third hole.

Swoop tried it on and with all the weight he'd lost from starvation this last month, it fit fairly well.

"Hmmm. Okay," he said, checking the sleeve length. Then he pulled the corpse by the arms about 50 yards away and down a slope. He knew soon, the timid and not so timid, paranoid bugs, animals and birds of the canyon lands would be sniffing the air, flying to and diving over and down and tiptoeing around, to eat it. Eating Sagiswatch.

Swoop lit a small fire, the leaves, twigs and branches already prepared for ignition. He removed the body-shaped, saddle-bag stuffings from the saddle and blanket and laid down where his replica body was once set up. He sat with his shoulders and neck up a bit by way of the saddle. He ate some of the jerky.

He looked at the small fire and up at the stars. The two horses were eating some grass side by side. Instant compadres. Sometime after dawn he would ride off north into Canada with not one but two horses and some supplies now, and some money. Maybe he'd find some work in Calgary. Lie low, but so far, laying low has not been his luck or fate.

But tonight he would rest. He'd done some really good deeds, saved a passel of kids from a life of hell, and now had some money, horses, supplies and spectacular place to sleep, and a plan for tomorrow. He could go around the world. But not in 80 days like Jules Verne thought possible.

Epilogue

Three weeks later...

Three U.S. Amy soldiers on horseback strolled eastbound on the river road with a small supply wagon behind them. They spotted the church-orphanage ahead. Major "Bare Eyes" Twenty looked to a lieutenant and sergeant next to him for a geographic update.

"According to the map, Major, this is the church," the lieutenant said.

"Hum. Like a fort," Major "Bare Eyes' Twenty said.

They rode closer. Two men in black, monk-like robes were struggling to set in place two new, big front wooden doors into a new frame.

"Can we help you gentlemen?" one stopped work and asked.

"Yes," Major Twenty said. "Can we speak to the man

in charge here?"

"Yes. That will be Father Calloway. Please just wait a second."

The three men dismounted and removed their riding gloves in unison. The Father appeared and introduced himself.

"How can we help you?" the priest asked.

"We are following up and making a report on the incidents that occurred here about a month ago," Major Twenty started. "You see, one of our most sought-after fugitives, a treasonous Lt. General Mordecai Swellen was here, and we are told he wreaked havoc upon this place."

"I was not here, sir," he said with a deep Irish accent. He pointed to the ground, "but only here but a mere week, sir. Me and the lads here. The place was empty. Like a ghost castle. Sent here from Chicago Archdiocese, we was. We only heard the story from the Archdiocese about what happened."

"What have you heard?"

"I don't think 'wreaking havoc' would be the best description for the man of which you speak, sir. That Swellen, known to them as Charles Last…was the man what rescued all these unfortunate kidnapped children from a life of prostitution. He was helped by the Wells Fargo and a United States Marshal, he was. Was this the man to whom you say was a traitor?"

"Yes."

"Well, maybe the goodness of our Lord has changed him since his traitor-isms? He sounds a bit like a saint, so the story goes. But, I know not of him any more than that."

"You have not heard rumors of his whereabouts? His destination?"

"As I told them lads what was here last week asking…"

"Asking? Lads? Last week? Who were they?"

"Cowboys they were. They were a calling themselves the Ditchmen, er Diggers, er…"

"Ditch…Diggers. Bounty hunters," Major Twenty offered up, "that's the name of their company."

"Must be them that be, yes, sir. The diggers of ditches of some sort. As I told them and now you, I have not a lick of knowledge about this man. Not one. He's long gone. And then we got here."

"May we have a look around Father. I have to file a report with the Army," Major twenty said.

"Oh, you may certainly do, sir. There is a barn and stable about halfway around back. Doors burned open like these here up front. Indians you know, the Archdiocese says. You can take the horses in through there.

"Do you know from whom the Archdiocese got all their information?"

"I believe that U.S, Marshal, sir."

"Calico Reems," Twenty said.

"I don't know the name."

"Stay here, Sergeant," Major Twenty told the wagon driver.

Major Twenty decided to walk, leading his mount by the reins. The other two officers followed. The wagon remained outside. They looked over the landscape and the pockmarked outer walls, worn and chipped from age, arrows and bullets. Then they walked through the burned doors of the barn. Once inside they wandered around the courtyard.

"Looks like one of our southwest forts, sir," the Lieutenant said.

"That it does, Louie," Major Twenty said. "No wonder Swoop protected it so well. Second nature. He's successfully protected a few in his day."

"Major, that swagger stick on your belt, did that once belong to Swoop Swellen?" The Lieutenant asked.

"Where did you hear that?"

"Just gossip, sir."

"Well, it was his once, yes."

"How'd you get it?"

"He left it in a Colorado hotel when he fled ahead of us, almost a year ago, now. I keep it, I wear it as a reminder that I must hunt him down. It is my main mission from General Shanklin. I will return it to Swellen someday. I plan on putting it in his coffin just before he's buried."

At that, the Lieutenant looked...skeptical.

THE END

If you haven't already, read Swoop's origin story,
Book 1 of the Renegade General

A series of gruesome murders occurred in Rocky Mountains of Canada. Murders so hideous that superstitious people even consider that the "Loup-Garou," the legendary wolfman beast is back on a rampage! The Royal Mounted Police barge into the Bar 18 Ranch House and deputize all 15 hands as posse members to chase the killer, the killers...or the monster. This forces their newest wrangler, Swoop Swellen into working closely with the Mounties on a man or beast hunt. Too closely...

The Johann Gunther Western Hero Adventure Series.   Ebooks, Paperback, Audio.

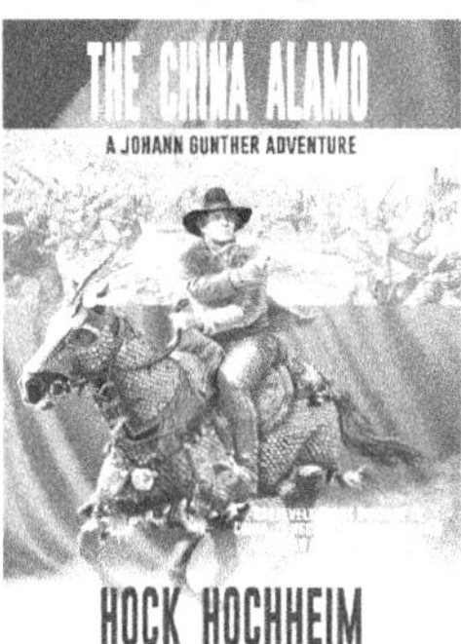

TRUTH IS DEADLIER THAN FICTION
DON'T EVEN THINK ABOUT IT
BOOK 1
TRUE STORIES OF CRIME AND JUSTICE
IN THE ARMY AND ON THE STREETS OF TEXAS
HOCK HOCHHEIM
TRUTH IS DEADLIER THAN FICTION
DEAD RIGHT THERE
BOOK 2
TRUE STORIES OF CRIME AND JUSTICE
IN THE ARMY AND ON THE STREETS OF TEXAS
HOCK HOCHHEIM